If You
See Me Comin'

If You See Me Comin'

ADRIAN MITCHELL

Allison & Busby
Published by W. H. Allen & Co. Plc

If you see me comin', sash your window high
If you see me comin', sash your window high
If you see me goin', hang your head and cry

(Blues)

An Allison & Busby book
Published in 1988 by
W. H. Allen & Co. Plc
44 Hill Street
London W1X 8LB

Printed and bound in Great Britain by
Cox & Wyman Ltd, Reading, Berkshire

ISBN 0 85031 812 2

CONTENTS

SUNDAY

THE UNSHAPELY leather bag was crammed with souvenirs
of things I didn't want to remember. It swung in my hand
as I stepped on to the grey slab platform of Belston station.
Specks of darkness were thickening in the air. Yellow buds
of light sprouted on the hills above the town and along the
edge of Belston Cliffs, cliffs which the sea had not fingered
for several million years. Tom, producer at the theatre,
stood nervously by the exit, peering for me. I am easy to
see. Few tall men of twenty-six have white hair and dark
eyes. But Tom, continuously swivelling his head as
travellers pushed by, did not see me. Why should he meet
me? Perhaps he thought I might not arrive, and perhaps
he was right. By his breast pocket he held his platform
ticket ostentatiously to assure himself and the public that
he was no trespasser. Rehearsals did not start for another
week. I had arrived early because I'd finished my month
at the Mingus Club and Belston is cheaper than London.
In three weeks' time I would be shouting the blues for
Tom in a revue called *Swing Low* (original title *This Show
Contains Silicones*), and on the first night Tom would be
conscientiously exposing his ticket to every programme
girl he could find. To save him any more pain, embarrass-
ment, apprehension, eyestrain, I yelled at him. He jumped,
so maybe I should have considered his nerves as well. We
shook hands while I wondered why you shake hands. To
show that you haven't got a sword in your right hand. But

7

I could have stabbed him with my left. It wouldn't have been fair though, he had no sword. He said 'Johnny,' and nodded about twenty-three times, while I thought of nothing but swords. Those swords were short and sharp, two-edged.

'Acorn Repertory,' Tom told the taxi-driver as I folded myself into the back seat. The driver slowly massaged his hair.

'What's that?'

'Acorn Repertory Theatre.'

'That in Mercy Street?'

Tom had to explain. The hum of his directions rose above and then fell below the murmur of the petrol-sipping engine. Tom joined me, nodding again.

'Are you going to be all right, Johnny?'

'Know my lines, and the songs—listen:

'Like an old subliminal advert
As it flashes on the screen,
You beat in my head from breakfast to bed
Though you're never heard or seen.
You're my tranquillizer in the morning
And my benzedrine at night.
I try to forget you, but I can't get you
Out of my mind though you're out of sight—'

Poor Tom looked cold, mainly because that was the worst song in the show, but he had to applaud my voice as good for a singer sitting in the back of a jerking taxi. He had to, because this bass voice living somewhere in my unpredictable stomach is both deep and flexible. At its happy wildest in a high-speed blues, it can carry cabaret junk or heavy-hearted ballads almost as easily. I hadn't made a disc, but I was a voice around the jazz clubs, a voice inside an unreliable man. When things get bad, I go somewhere else.

'Voice sounds fine, Johnny. But how do you feel?'

8

'Count my corpuscles. Look, I know I was pretty beat down when I left last year, but things are good now.'

I told two half-lies when I said that. 'Pretty beat down' meant that I screeched to a halt just short of a breakdown, and 'things are good now' meant that I hadn't felt sick all day.

A long road leads from the station to the centre of Belston, one edge lined with telegraph poles. I know Belston. Belston is English, with a dying market, cliffs, two large factories, a shallow, industrially-useful river, one minor university, and a history which is noble compared with the history of some other towns. It used to be defended by a wall of local stone. Now its guardians are forty-eight members of Civil Defence, most of them housewives who practise the stewing of mutton on open-air stoves. When the bomb comes they plan to whitewash their windows. After a year at the Acorn playing Americans, there were more people I liked in that town than anywhere else in the world, but I knew that if the chance came they would regretfully nail a Christ to each of those telegraph poles. A few of them, the extremists who used the Acorn as their coffee-bar, might start a protest march with banners saying SAVE THE THIEVES — NOW, but most of the citizens would turn out on their bikes or in their Sunday-polished cars for the ceremony. A lovely day for a picnic on the hills, what a pity it had to get dark so soon. Pity it had to get suddenly dark.

It was getting darker and Tom mumbled through one of the revue tunes. I could make out the rhythm as he talked the notes. I wondered what he would be doing at the next Calvary; then I stopped, because I hate predicting what people are going to do. You feel responsible for them if you are right, unfair if you are wrong. Once I met a reporter who was covering an ecclesiastical conference and he swore all the time. I could guess what I would be doing at the next Calvary; I'd be doing singing, doing drinking, doing no good at all.

'Anything worrying you, Johnny?'

'Not a thing. I'm just furrowing my brows. It's my gimmick.'

Another lie. I was worried. Next Saturday morning, as the morning began, they were going to hang this man McAllen. I didn't know McAllen. I had only read about him, seen his photograph, his face constructed of dots on the coarse paper, his eyes, the highlights of his eyes, the arrowed picture of the haystack where he did it. I didn't know him, but I don't like people being hanged. I noticed that I was beating the arm of my seat with a white fist, so I fiddled for cigarettes. When you blow smoke in a jet at glass it spreads, then falls in on itself in waves. You can watch a sideshow like that for seconds and make believe it matters. Outside the theatre Tom counted his change while I counted my feet. I had two feet. The taximan examined the small theatre designed in the most daring modern idiom—like Clara Bow the It Girl—and read aloud its sign.

'The Acorn Repertory Theatre. Huh. Great oaks from little acorns grow.'

'What?' I asked.

'Great Oaks from Little Acorns Grow, it's a quotation, you're educated. Hope you don't put on a-corny show. Ha ha.' He laughed. 'Ha ha.' He laughed some more, literally saying ha ha; some people do. I laughed too, in an intelligent sort of way, giving his rear bumper a playful kick and turning to Tom.

'Hear that? Hear that one, Tom? Great Oaks—'

'Heard it,' he said, deducting sixpence from the tip. We stamped down the ally to the stage door, passing children as they played an old Belston street game, now, alas, dying out in this age of mass-communication, space rockets and Soggo, the Silent Breakfast Cereal. You get a piece of chalk and put it on the pavement and then you keep jumping on it. Then you get another piece of chalk. A broken chalk flew out and hit my shoe. It was purple, so I autographed a paving stone for the kids—Johnny Crane—you can't do too much for the fans. At the stage door I turned, and there in the alley was a thin girl standing over my name staring at me, black eyes in a face as dazzling white as the element in a light bulb. Her mouth was pulling down at the corners, she looked like someone seeing a killed man for the first time, her face whiter than the stars. I wanted to say something reassuring, but what can you say that doesn't sound pernicious in a brown alley? My mouth opened, but said nothing. She was running, a silhouette dragging a shadow behind her as she ran to the lamplit street. Behind her two woollen infants continued to push each other about, a small boy smoked intensely and his sister jumped up and down on chalk.

As I walked through the stage door a hand patted me on the head. It was the soft right hand of Velma. I acted Leonato to her Beatrice in the old days, last season I mean. She pats everyone, the world is her poodle.

'Have some salad sandwiches, Johnny,' she said. 'My dressing-room is full of them.'

'They treat the theatre like a rabbit hutch,' Tom said, walking down the splintering steps to the stage. On Velma's dressing-table were two triangular sandwiches, beginning to curl with age. Round the corner of the L-shaped room was a muffled noise that was probably a colleague changing sweaters. Like a gentleman, I kept my eyes on the sandwiches. Velma placed her hands on my shoulder pads. She has a way with her, whether you like it or not.

'Have you heard about Elspeth, Johnny?'

'No. How is she?'

'Nobody knows. Thursday afternoon she didn't come in. We rehearsed another scene and she still didn't come in.'

'You went on without her? That's like playing Hamlet without the Second Gravedigger. But Elspeth's reliable. Where was she?'

'We don't know. I've had to take over her part.'

'Loyal girl,' I said. Velma tweaked my ears. 'Maybe she got married.'

From out of sight, round the corner of the room, a

cobbled voice. Roger Blester was sitting in a corner so that his back was to two walls at once. He said:

'She might as well be dead.'

Velma always looked shocked by Roger. He was invariably working as a temporary barman, he was never permanent. He moved through Belston stealthily, with insulting certainty, like a disciple walking, for the second time, on water. Ex-communist, ex-anarchist, ex-social animal, he had become a one-man political party dedicated to the overthrow of everything he could get his hands on. A lay preacher of destruction whose faith was reserved for his own personality, he never looked at people. That was why he frightened almost all those who met him, because they felt they meant nothing to him. He would launch, fuelled with drink, into a sky-high monologue, nearly always leaning against something, mantelpiece or bar, rubbing his hands over his face and hair as he talked. He scared people, and the scare lasted after they had forgotten that he was short and blunt-nosed, a noisy, sharp-tongued shadow in the corner of a room. I knew he stole, but only from big institutions which could afford it, like railway stations and cathedrals.

'She might as well be dead,' he said. 'Like our great-grandmothers, she has been replaced. Like them, she has left no forwarding address. Oration. Nor was she blonde, nor was she tall, nor was she distinguished, no, my friends. But she was—a woman. How did she pass? Was it the director's Bentley speeding back from the country-club dinner, or the pack of motor-cyclists on the 108th turning on the way home from a rally? Was it the hand of the Almighty which smote her down, or the boot of a sex-maniac maddened by the moon of her face? Was it mayhem or matrimony? We make questions to the stars and the answers are written in last year's tea-leaves, now decomposed. How shall we mourn her? Not with the marble memorial and the florid tribute, not with the final furnace and the hand of an underpaid, underfed youth on the bellows of the weeping organ, but by ordering one too many cups

12

of coffee, by forgetting to announce her replacement before the curtain rises, by calling Velma "Elspeth" occasionally.'

I put a waste-paper basket over his head and something behind me snarled. Roger said 'Leave him, boy,' and the huge St. Bernard which had been lurking under the table mumbled as it nosed the basket off his head and licked his nose with a lively tongue. Roger's hands began to pat the dog, with the firmness and regularity of a bongo drummer. His eyes half closed and he was thinking of nothing but the young dog. It was both powerful and beautiful, its white fur very white, its brown almost gold, its eyes the size of the eyes of the dog in the fairy-tale. His paws were as large as children's slippers.

'What do you call him?' I asked.

Roger looked up furiously, his eyes narrower than usual. I had interrupted a silent, private conversation.

'I call him God,' he said. 'He's the only perfect being I know. He is all honesty. His instincts are as pure as the driven detergent. He does not beat his chest and lie awake in the daytime like Walt Whitman. He has no use for money, it has the wrong smell. The friends I've got can be numbered on the fingers of one foot. But I need protection, everyone does. Some people get friendly with the old God and give him prayers in return for an unreliable sort of insurance. I give this dog plenty of food and get real protection. Another reason for calling him God is that God happens to be Dog spelled backwards. I don't keep him so that I can give him orders, I'm no policeman. I trained him, and he never goes on a lead. If he wants to come with me, he comes; if he doesn't, he sleeps at home. He doesn't disapprove of anything, he is a tolerant, big God.'

'You want to get your brain washed,' said Velma. 'And Johnny, you want to get your face fed. You're getting even thinner.' She pinched my ribs.

'We'll get a snack and leave these leaf sandwiches for Roger,' I said.

13

I remembered the paper in my jacket and took it out. I'd only collected four signatures for McAllen's reprieve, two of them from singing football fans on the Underground. Roger looked at the paper.

'Capital punishment is all right, but they hang the wrong people. You don't want my name, the Home Secretary knows about me. I wrote to him last week asking him to bring back the cat for corrupt police inspectors.'

With Velma I walked across to the Unicorn for food, the pub where Roger should have been working. It's a compact pub, completely surrounded by tall buildings with windowless walls. As it faces no street, you have to walk down a steep passage paved with small grey stones, past a full-flowering bombed site to reach it. You can sing as loud as you like in the Unicorn, there are no neighbours to complain. Though the building is small, the two bars are long, wide and uninhibited, with matt wood floors, a piano which once almost burnt down, a neat bar billiards table with only one tear in the cloth, and a tiled backyard with hollyhocks for the summer. There are stools so high your head brushes the distemper off the ceiling, and armchairs so relaxed that your bum hits the floor. Lampshades are nicotined and ineffectual, made of stitched parchment, and the bulbs are strong, so that faces gain hard, character-granting shadows as the evening outside darkens to the colour of a Guinness. Multicoloured Christmas lights shine on their string all day long, all the year round.

An owl-faced man looked at me as if he recognized me and didn't like me. I looked back. I didn't recognize him, but I didn't like him for not liking me. Currents of mutual dislike passed between us, then we both switched off and never looked each other in the eyes again. Behind the longer bar, the exotic bottles of Trinidad liqueurs and local potato wine contemplating themselves in the long engraved mirrors and flashing intermittent invitations from their shelves, stood the stooping landlord Dave, too thin you would think ever to be granted a licence, too

14

contemptuous you might imagine to keep a single customer. Velma and I side-stepped like a dance team to let Roger and God pass to their places behind the bar.

'What are you having? Are you buying them, actor?'

The three of us had large bitters. Then Roger was called to the other end of the bar by two creamy young men with clean hats on. I heard the beginning of his attack on them, his harsh voice softening into a quiet wheedle.

'Two gin and bitter lemons, yes, and can I persuade you to try a packet of Cheese Fancies each? Only sixpence.'

'No thank you very much,' said the taller of the two, turning his tailored back to the bar.

'Only sixpence,' said Roger. 'They contain proteins. I think they'd suit you two young gentlemen. Do you a world of good. Tell you what, try one out of my packet with no obligation.'

'No thank you, could we have our gins?'

'But they help to keep you thirsty, very salty, you appreciate your drinks more.'

'No.'

Roger sighed and produced the drinks. The shorter man paid with a five pound note. Roger looked at it edgeways on for some time before changing it. Velma put her hand on my arm.

'It's good, isn't it?' she said.

I didn't know what she meant was good, Roger's act, the beer, the two of us drinking together again, the two of us being together again, or even the quality of Cheese Fancies. So I said:

'How does Roger hold down this job? Must be six months since I was here last and he still serves an insult with every drink. I bet he gets in fights after closing time.'

'He's got that dog. Dave kicked him out once. Roger was lecturing a vicar about temperance and making up quotations from St Paul. But the vicar wanted to continue the argument and he pleaded so much that Dave took Roger back.'

'Is the vicar here?'

15

'No. Roger told him his theory about the Royal Family. He doesn't come any more. But by that time Dave had had enough of the vicar and his habits, so he let Roger stay. Let's move on somewhere else, Johnny.'

'Let's eat first.'

Roger tried to sell us Cheese Fancies.

'They're my bread and butter,' he whined. 'Tell you what, I've got some extra-special French Cheese Fancies under the counter just for you. Collectors' pieces they are.'

'I think you're annoying the young lady.'

'Why not? She's my young lady now.'

I gave him an imitation glare and Velma's hand tightened on my sleeve. She is always hanging on to your clothes or your flesh.

'Don't joke,' she said. 'You're my nothing.'

'They all say that. They all say that,' said Roger, looking at his hands. 'And it always ends the same way. The pupils return from the school treat, tired but happy.'

'I'm not playing,' said Velma. 'Not with you anyway.'

'Wait and see,' said Roger, and disappeared below the level of the bar to find us some black and brown pasties. After another bitter Velma wanted to stay.

'It's my magnetism,' said Roger. 'The doctors were shocked by it when I was born. Velma, you will be mine.'

He vanished again. We found a corner seat and I knew she was going to ask why I didn't write. I didn't write because I only wanted to say something to Velma when she was with me, and even then what I wanted to say was simple, too simple to say. We communicated, imperfectly, with our hands. Our minds, when they met, didn't often agree, but our bodies had similar opinions.

'You didn't write.'

'I was struggling, Velma. I was working hard, but when I wasn't working I was sick. I get sick, you know. If I'd written to people it would have been like being sick on them. I wanted to be forgotten for a time. But thanks for the letters.'

16

I read one of her letters. That one upset me. For three pages it was full of facts about the theatre, good solid facts, then it dissolved into a mess of sympathy on the last page. Sympathy is for drunks.

'Was it your leg, Johnny?'

It wasn't my leg. I caught a bit of shrapnel in Korea and it gave me an occasional limp, but that didn't make me sick.

'No.'

'Can I do anything for you, Johnny?'

'Honest, I don't think I'm much good for you, love. We'd better not strike up the band again.'

I found it hard to look at her, so pretty and anxious, a girl in love with my voice. I could understand her; I love my voice, the best part of me. It had been a slow, occasionally stormy affair, with most of the complications on my side. Why not go to bed? Johnny is sick tonight, he wants to go walking all night alone, walking all the next day, walking till he's too tired to see out of his eyes. Why not get married? Johnny gets sick, marriage could make him sicker. Why not go out together for a drink? Johnny hasn't turned up, where is he, nobody knows, expect he's sick somewhere, in some library, pub or ditch. Or maybe he's in his room, just being scared of being sick. I'll tell you what makes me sick. All this killing. They showed me in Korea. That reminded me of the McAllen petition, so I brought it out and shook off the tobacco grains.

'I'd rather not sign,' Velma said.

Dave signed it. The two creamy men looked at it, and the taller one said Great Heavens No with an exclamation mark. Roger signed Elizabeth Regina. A man with hairy ears said he never signed anything, another said he had to be careful, another said it wouldn't do any good. I avoided the owl man and returned to Velma.

'I'm sorry, Johnny, I'd like to, but I don't know much about it. And doesn't the Government keep all the names and it makes getting an American visa difficult?'

17

Velma didn't know much about it.

'Forget it.'

'No, but I do agree with it really, but I don't see that my name, well, you know—'

'Forget it.'

There was a pause. Then she said: 'Where are you sleeping?'

She looked fine and sleepy. Her yellow hair curled like feathers all over her perched head. The fingers of her left hand were flexing between the fingers of my right. Out of habit our hands bumped from my thigh to hers and back again. The band was striking up. Because I was pleased I gargled with beer and she giggled. Once Velma laughs there is no stopping her, and nobody would want to stop her.

'Not sure,' I said. As we left, Roger said: 'Velma,' and he extended the fingers of one hand in farewell.

She had moved to a new room. It was so frilled and feminine that I felt embarrassed, like shopping for petticoats on a Monday morning in a big store. The low-wattage bulbs were over-shaded, the music cool, the night air sultry; hastily-eaten pasties cause indigestion. Under the little window a drunk was singing the Clifton School song:

> 'We'll honour yet the School we knew,
> The best school of all.
> We'll honour yet the rule we knew
> Till the last bell call.
> For working days and holidays
> And glad or melancholy days,
> They were great days and jolly days
> At the best School of all.'

Like a child, Velma took me by the hand to show me round the four corners of the room. Even the books were in pastel colours. From the radiogram flowed, tinkled and chimed the Modern Jazz Quartet. Shallow yellow carpet covered the floor. Above the electric fire was a hand-

18

coloured photograph of a man in uniform. He looked excessively cheerful, ready to laugh his way out of the frame.

'Who's that?'

I remembered Bessie Smith pleading, stretching out her voice like a grasping brown hand: 'All I want is your picture, It must be in a frame.'

'My brother Robert.'

"I've got a brother and a sister but I don't keep them in frames.'

'He was killed at Tripoli.'

Among all that sand. The air was gritty with the sharp yellow stuff. Finding a dead man, the sand first formed an extra skin for him, then another layer and then another, until it had constructed a smooth barrow for him. I had forgotten that people call the dead by name. For the first time in a week I anticipated nausea. Velma had to tell me all about Robert before I was calm again.

'Now forget Robert,' she said eventually, touching my coarse white hair. 'Nearly everyone's forgotten him and you never even knew him. You look plain silly, as if you're going to cry.'

'I know I look plain silly. All that sand. Talk about something else. I know, how about signing this petition?'

'I've told you, Johnny, I'd rather not.'

'You will, won't you, come on, love, I've only got five genuine signatures. One more, just one, and I get a silver badge with "I Eat Soggo with a Good Conscience" engraved on it. Just your little name, Velma, write it quick, I promise not to look.'

'What's Soggo?'

I'm bad at logic at any time, and her long arms round my neck made it impossible to think straight. My unrelieved view of fair curls made ethics unthinkable. I tried.

'It's the new wonder cereal in the black pack. Try it with fruit salts. Look, love, revenge is for cretins—'

Her arms pulled me tighter until our mouths jammed against each other. Her embrace was somehow firm, passive and all-permissive. My hands began to wander and so did

19

my thoughts. I wondered what Elspeth, that dull girl, was doing. I didn't care, I just wondered because wondering is my habit. I mentally counted my cigarettes and decided I had enough for the morning if Velma only smoked two. I discounted the idea that Velma might have cigarettes of her own. I thought I heard a soldier marching by in the street. I patted my inside pocket to assure myself I still had the packet from the chemist's. My eyes were shut, my head full of colours. Velma wanted to be undressed, and vaguely I resented this, painfully impatient by now. When the grey pullover was dragged over her head she looked like some new creature being born. Her lilac bra cast lilac reflections on her white waist. There were three books by Georgette Heyer by the bed. I had to go to the lavatory because of the beer. Everything seemed so easy, even if it might soon seem meaningless. We neither talked, nor laughed, nor cried. My clothes were a jumbled heap of shadows on the floor, the record stopped itself. It was a sober love-making, we learnt nothing new. There was a pause. I felt cold air from a gap at the bottom of the window touch my face. We moved apart. I lumbered over to my jacket, pulled out my revue script, and silently hollered the songs. Velma slept, smiling, beside me. I felt hollow, threw down the script and encircled her. We slept. Her dreams were good. My dreams were bad.

MONDAY

WINDOWS CONTROL a room. Light adjusts our moods.
Rain down the glass can be invigorating as bitter down the
throat. Morning sun has the hand of a woman. But the
thick brown curtains were closed over Velma's window. I
woke suddenly because I was scared that it was Saturday
and McAllen was dropping from life into death as I was
falling from sleep into the day. Then my memory said
Monday, it must be Monday, and my watch said eight
o'clock, too early. Velma's wrist lay along my furred leg.
I slid to the floor, pulled on her dressing-gown and lit up.
By now my eyes were adapted to the new day, so I padded
along the lino to the bathroom.

As the water fell rustily I decided not to think about
McAllen. Velma was a prettier thought. Thinking about
Velma's personality without Velma's body was a failure.
Thinking of Velma's personality plus her body was too
complex, her personality might contain remarkable hidden
byways, but they were mostly unexplored. I thought about
her body. It was all welcome friend, but there was no
frenzy in it. The bath filled and I softened my feet in its
tropical waters. A bath softens my head too, and I saw myself as a ragged man with a Jesus beard, toting a tailor's
dummy in a sack on my shoulder and being unjustly arrested
every mile of my pilgrimage to Whitehall, Moscow or
Washington.

I decided to sing my head clear. I ran through a gentle, thirty-one-verse treatment of Frankie and Johnny. The bartender sounded like Louis Armstrong and I used Sarah Vaughan tricks for Frankie's comments. Johnny died with a metallic death-rattle. She shot him through that hardwood door, and I kept my eyes on the door. At the pace of a funeral Daimler I took 'Bring out your rubber-tyred hearses'. My favourite verse is:

> The Judge he said to Frankie
> Explain it if you can.
> Frankie looked him straight in the eye
> Said I shot my lovin' man,
> He was my man, and he done me wrong.

It has the simplicity of a desert stone that blows unloved away and becomes one with wind, sand, stars and William Wordsworth. Above my head the bulb was bare and bright. Below my head my body was bare and pink. My head was the centre of the bathroom. Before my eyes swung sharp green shapes, spikes and crescents, because the bulb was so bare and so bright. By the time I reached Frankie and Johnny's moral, someone was knocking. It was the red and white body of Velma, come to collect its bath. In her bedroom I smoked and read the small ads in the *Melody Maker*. Sun fell between the chimneys opposite, out of the sky and in through the window. I caught it gratefully as it splashed across the bed. It fell gently until I tried to look into the eye of the sun, then I had to clench my eyelids. I could see only a golden red blur. I thought, there won't be any letters, nobody knows I'm here, except maybe Roger. When I was at private school in Los Angeles for a year, I used to pray, when I did pray, for a letter every morning. I wrote to all the people I knew and to some people I knew only because they were famous. Each day I wrote down the number of letters received, but the most I ever got was four on my birthday, and that was five less than Chris Ferrars, who sat next to me at breakfast, had more money and more dandruff than me, and never wrote letters at all.

A boxed note in the *Melody Maker* suddenly became clear and important. 'The recently-formed Ben Lewis Trio now plays nightly for diners at the International Hotel, Belston. Mr Charles Dickson, new proprietor, says: "This is the first time jazz has been heard at the International, we hope to make it a regular attraction, pull in the younger set. Primarily the Trio will play restrained rhythm for dancers." Line-up remains Lewis (piano), Bob Blackburn (bass) and Flak Peters (drums). Flight Records will issue the Trio's first disc, two Lewis originals, in early autumn.'

Ben Lewis—the very name was like a ball. When I ladled out sad, bad ballads for Ronnie Johnson, the debutante's dilemma, Ben was the band's weather-beaten pianist, only he told me the tan was nicotine, not weather. After an evening of songs Ivor Novello's mother taught him, Ben and I used to shake it all away with the hard, fast blues and strong ale. Ben can talk, but he chooses not to, letting his fingers do the talking. Ben in Belston was the first I had heard of him for three months. He must be my closest friend, and our relationship was always the same; when we met we made music.

When Velma suggested a cup of tea, I remembered I was due to visit my sister Joan for breakfast. Velma went back to bed and turned over in a drowsy hump of sulk as I left to see journalist Joan Crane, thirty, sane-brained, Celtic-svelte, happily divorced. She reports and runs a woman's column for the *Belston Gazette*. She can capture any dress or hat in one high-heeled phrase—an Empire dream of tulle in Lieutenant-Colonel puce, a cellar-black Nefertiti sandal. Her advice is dogmatic:

OFF-BEAT BEAUTY

KEEP your tongue smooth by rolling and unrolling it. Contrast its natural blood-colour by using a creamy green stick on your upper lip, pale crimson on your lower . . . FOR the woman who's different in the nicest possible way—men's shirts and ties handpainted with portraits of Mr Universe or Old Testament characters . . . WHITE prayer-books for the Great Day of course, but you never thought of rebinding that tatty old family Bible to match your accessories for cathedral-going, did you? . . . MADLY gay is the new Free Expression Studio near St Pancras, where amateurs tattoo each other—well worth a trip to the Smoke . . . QUITE irresistible—the new 'Noose' necklaces fashioned by trusties at prisons favoured by the professional classes . . . NICKNAMES are part of popularity—put a ring through your nose and ask your friends to call you 'Piggy' . . .

Reaching Joan's flat from Velma's was an easy journey, straight across the flat face of the park. Already bulky boys occupied all the swings, travelling higher and higher, counting down each time their seats waited for an instant motionless at the end of a double arc. Ten—nine—eight. And with zero—fire!—each boy let go of his chains and hurtled through the air, beyond the tarmac on to the clipped grass. Along the paths a man in a damp-looking blue uniform swept aside decaying litter and a few leaves which might offend the delicate. As he swept he swore to a small congregation of birds, solemn and philosophical foreign ducks, mean sparrows and a few burning robins. They were all chewing the carpet of breadcrumbs he had laid for them.

'I don't mind you lot, you bloody birds, you don't leave much mess, you don't bust up the roundabout, you don't hide in the bushes when I lock up, you don't misbehave all over the bowling green. Have you got a light?'

I gave him a light, and he started to tell me about his illness.

'I shouldn't be doing this, with my chest, everyone says I shouldn't. I shouldn't be here at all. With my chest.' He looked at me as if my shirt was solid gold. 'I wish I was your age,' he said. 'I wish I was happy.'

There was nothing I could do, so I walked on and into the smart, oblong block of flats. Joan was cooking bacon

24

and eggs. I sat at the table, picked up a square of dark toast, smeared it with butter and honey and began to munch. In pyjamas and a towelly dressing-gown, hair stitched into curlers, holding a frying-pan with a chipped wooden handle, Joan grinned. That grin shone.

'How's the old Acorn?' she asked.

'Do we talk at breakfast?'

'I just like to know everything. I won't print anything.'

'Velma hasn't changed, Tom seems jumpy about the revue—'

'Just tell me the births, deaths and marriages.'

'Elspeth vanished. About three days ago and nobody knows where.'

'That's all, I suppose.'

'I suppose. Nobody seems to know any more. She hasn't written.'

'Set of actors. So you just leave it at that.'

'Roger thought she was dead.'

'Roger thinks everyone is dead. He'll be lynched one day. He forges letters from the Mayor to the *Gazette*. Did anyone try to find out where Elspeth went?'

'You mean we should be out with bloodhounds and flaming torches?'

'I don't mean you should care, but you might show some interest. Perhaps she wasn't very interesting.'

Joan was right. Elspeth, with a formal brand of beauty, was so explicable, so easily ignored. She looked before she leaped, thought before she spoke, made up before she went out, and considered before she laughed. Every night she gave the same performance, whatever the play. Nobody thought she would ever do anything exceptional, unkind or interesting.

'I think she just went somewhere else. She might imagine that changing towns would change her character. I remember the night she expressed an opinion. She called Belston dull.'

'Elspeth wouldn't leave without telling Tom.'

'She hated rows, any kind of emotion. She wouldn't have

25

told him, she'd have left a note. But she wouldn't have mislaid it. Someone else might have dropped it, not Elspeth. She must have given it to someone unreliable who forgot it.'

I felt in my pockets. There was no note.

'Forget it,' said Joan. 'Forget it. Just show a little more concern if the earth swallows me up one day. Johnny, will you take me to the ball on Friday night? A wild party, the Mayor's own. It lost £260 for charity last year. I've got complimentaries. All I have to do is write a few captions. But I don't want to be stuck with one partner for the night.'

I nodded soberly. He must be a man she didn't know well enough yet, or a married man. There was a chance that I could sing at the ball and it was worth taking.

'I'll come.'

'And come round again for breakfast. That's the only time I'm alone,' she said. 'Now, will you be all right, Johnny? I mean, how are things?'

'You mean, my mind?'

She nodded and cleared the cups, holding away from me. Her tough hazel eyes water easily.

'I should be all right,' I said quickly. 'Yes, yes. You know, I'm getting this trouble about McAllen. Will you sign this reprieve thing?'

She pointed to the sideboard. Her copy of the petition bore two columns full of names.

'I'll be all right,' I said, and tap-danced out of the flat to demonstrate how all right I would be.

An outsize imagination is useful but disturbing. I can make the top of my brain green and fine like a spring field even when I'm on a bench in a smoke-infested railway station. It can be good to be a field. You lie with your wide green acres, and when the rain comes down you like it, you like the plants growing on you. I can make snow come down, evenly whitening the field. Or I can plough up that detailed surface of grass and clover, leaving an area of deep earth, full of underearth creatures, like a solid sea. More usefully, I can sweat confidence when the seven-foot brigands hold their knives at my throat. On stage I use the trick. I get to know the character better than the lines, so I could improvise for pages if they let me.

But the newspapers are terrible. Because reading the papers is my personal fiery furnace, I try to ignore them, but they demand to be read, the headlines cry to me. The front page, and there are floods in China. The yellow dust is bullied into mud, high waves of mud sweep down the villages to shipwreck the houses and tear away the small goods of the dust-coloured people. If I read long enough, I have to do something, like selling a lighter or a suitcase, to send small change to China, to the man like myself in that yellow wave in China, and the wave of mud rolls through my dreams for weeks. There's always the sports page—I glow from the praises of the generous writers, I glower under the lash of the vicious hack, promising myself to ride, play, jump, swim, golf and fight better next time. Reports from the front I leave alone. I buried dead things like people in Korea. We had to be drunk to do it. I can't read about wars. I read about murders. I think I understand them because I was burying those dead people. The first time I went out with the lorry they said I could watch. Some of them vomited while they worked. The worst part of murders in the papers is the announcement of the execution date. They tell you when it will be, to the minute. I think more and more about the hanging until the night itself, spending the days and nights fending off the breakdown I fear. Sometimes I escape it with drink. Sometimes I try to hide from everyone.

I decided to leave that man McAllen behind me for the time being, so I rounded the street corner like Charlie Chaplin. Straight ahead was a telephone box. I dialled Velma. Using the double ring as a rhythm section, I hummed my own arrangement of 'How High the Moon' into the mouthpiece.

'Are you fine, Velma, are you fine?'

She was still yawning.

'Fine,' she said.

'Look, this big dance on Friday. I've got a free ticket

27

but it's only for one. I'll probably be drunk or something. Shall I get another for you?'

A pause from Velma.

'Johnny, it's a bit difficult. You see, I promised to go with someone else before you came back to town. You see, it was a promise.'

'Never mind. See you there anyway.'

'Before then. Tonight. What are you doing?'

'Going to read the papers.'

'All day?'

'Maybe. Who's taking you to this dance?'

'Roger. He's on one of the bars so he gets a ticket. I suppose we'll get a few dances together. I'm sorry, Johnny, I want to be honest with you.'

'Christ, you don't need to worry, girl. Velma, you are fine, I dig you like mad, don't worry. We never said anything about ownership, or love for that matter.'

'We agreed about that—'

'That night in the bathroom.'

'Yes.'

'Sure. Fine, then, love to you.'

We hung up on each other agreeably and I felt good and independent again. I was blowing on the glass panels of the booth, drawing Velma and ducks on alternate windows in the mist, when the door swung open. A wedge-faced woman confronted me, her arms folded.

'What's all this?'

'A telephone box.'

'What do you think you're doing in it?'

'I happen to be an official from Telephone House, a plain-clothes telephone-box inspector, a kiosk-scrutinizer, and I was testing the glass of Box 4923 for intrinsic flaws. Do you realize that the condensation of the human breath on the glass of a kiosk can, by the change in temperature induced, cause the loosening, and in extreme cases the explosion, of the glass? We have received complaints, madam, we have received complaints.'

28

I looked at her sternly but her glare did not shift. I moved out, she in. I finished my drawings on the outside and left her, still trying to get through to someone who had the sense to be out. There was nothing for it but the public library, up the hill, to read the papers. There might be a reprieve for McAllen; that thought always whispered to me when a man had been condemned. The Library, with hippopotamus domes and pillars like the legs of elephants, was built by one of the clumsier nineteenth-century men as a rival to any other possible or impossible civic edifice. Its carvings of flat-chested nymphs in relief have a certain leerworthy charm. On either side of the steps are lamp-posts in black barley-sugar. I tried to concentrate that small circle, the gun-sight of my brain, on the unwieldy body of the building, but already the back of my neck was too hot or too cold. The song in my head was being dried up by other thoughts. I had to see the papers. Of course it would be wiser to sit by the magazine rack and read something harmless like the *Wasp-Fanciers' Quarterly* or the *Shadow-Boxer's Friend*, better to go back to Velma, any foolish deliverance. My foot in the gutter hit a tree's branch. It was lying there, ownerless as myself, about eight feet long, so I picked it up, stood it on one end and stared at it. It had been part of a silver birch; wrist thin at the top, thigh thick at the bottom. I could have left it propped against the green railings of the churchyard, to improve the view of off-white tombstones, but I knew the other walkers in the street would crash it into the gutter again.

I laid the thick end in the gutter, grasped the thin end and walked on, accompanied now by a bouncing branch with the spring of a dog in its white length. It leapt from the road to the pavement and back again while I took three strides. Carefully dragged, it ploughed lifelessly through mud and water, but with a flick of my wrist a watersplash rose to hang in the air and light for a second. A besuited man, well-shaven and grey, began to pass me with his round eyes looking straight through my neck, an unpleasant feeling. A short chain of water beads suddenly decorated him from his waist to the heels of his shoes, without his noticing, as the branch jived a few inches into the air. I prepared myself for a middle-aged galleon who sailed towards me towing a dinghy dog, puffing herself along with her own perfumed wind, but as I gripped the branch I saw two of my friends across the street, both serious Indian undergraduates. I couldn't hide the branch, it was eight feet of evidence against me. I continued to drag it as if it were injured, in need of repair; they smiled at me and we all shouted good morning simultaneously and then laughed, as if something was funny. I kept my hold on the branch.

At the Library I parked it alongside the steps and loped up to the glass revolving doors. One of my accomplishments, learnt perhaps while evacuated and playing American football, is that I can sprint down a pavement at its most crowded and, by swivelling my hips, throw my weight an inch to one side of the oncoming old lady. On steps I am even more spectacular; three hundred performances in the top-hat chorus of a West End revue taught me more about steps than I like to remember.

Inside the Library the floors were polished like Heaven. In the Reference Room I took down a copy of *Kine Weekly* and pretended to read. Outside the Library there was some air and a sun; inside, the lamps were on, standing on their tables as they will always stand. Men in sports coats, thick fingers folded against their foreheads, were writing with quick, angry ball-point pens, their lips twisted in attitudes of righteous indignation. I read one sentence. The girls, shining with enlightened self-interest, unconscious of their breasts, sat calmly over their books, most of them beautiful, reading and waiting for nothing to happen. Nothing did happen. The notices proclaimed S I L E N C E in fat letters, but the floor was ideal for roller-skating. Slowly the dust descended from the high, probably bat-bearing rafters, coursing down my throat, settling in my stomach, inflaming my liver. This is a dry aquarium, I thought. Or this is an Academy painting of the Library, Belston, and these are painted people at painted tables reading painted books. Or the world has at least come to its end, there is nothing outside the Library, no street, no town, no world, no branch, no Velma. This is the way the world ends, with the scholars feverishly annotating the last page of creation.

Beginning to frighten myself, I changed the subject, glancing over the rows of good advice in the reference books. Books bother me. I used to want to pile them into skyscrapers, each tower a different subject, and diligently climb each tower. That was when I was fourteen, and from an early excess of fat my face was thinning intelligently. At fifteen I gave up reading and began singing. At sixteen I wanted to burn those piled books in a mile-high bonfire to thaw out the cold girls. Now that the unread pile is higher than ever, I would rather watch it, reading interesting titles, just as I prefer watching mountains to climbing them.

But the titles seemed dull, the cold was in my stomach again, the dust and the calm of the humans about me made it worse. I crossed the hall and opened the door of the newspaper room. The only other reader was a bundle of sacks tied together with a stolen macintosh, an oval head of ash-coloured hair surmounting fallen shoulders as he read aloud to himself from the *Daily Mirror* city column. In the first paper I chose there was nothing about McAllen. Instead I followed the progress of science, without which how could toothpaste be striped? The headline said 'Scalp Flakes':

The connection between dandruff and lawn-mowing is now definitely proven, claims Dr Arnold Weggis in this week's issue of *Scalpel*.

98-year-old, Leamington Spa-born Dr Weggis, who takes size seven in suede, plastic-soled shoes, has spent 17 years, £890 11s. 7d. on research. Volunteers, all students from the Guildhall School of Music and Drama, mowed his Putney lawn ten hours a day, four days a week.

31

Result of the research—81 per cent of the men who went to mow either contracted dandruff or had it when they started. 73·52 per cent of the controls either did not contract dandruff or had dry scalp anyway. Eight per cent of the mowers were bald.

But I report fierce opposition to the doctor's thesis. Today the 19-year-old President of the Lawn-Mower Manufacturers' Guild, Mr Honest Jim Colby, told me 'What goes on in the mind of a man like old Weggis is beyond my comprehension, probably beyond his. In the days when he had a flat above Palme Dutt's he used to entertain a great many actors.

'I have never touched a lawn-mower in my life and I have plenty of dandruff. I have sent some of it to Weggis. When you next see the old boy you might ask him about his little sister. I'd be interested to hear what he has to say about her.'

My Harley Street friends are undecided on the Weggis theory, give me this advice—play safe, oil your mower with hair tonic.

The opposite page carried an advertisement for the Permanent Royal Bank of England Ecclesiastical Building Society. I would sooner put my money in Jolly Jack's Soho Christmas Club. The next paper was the one. Those words again, repeating that McAllen would hang on Saturday morning, eight o'clock. I thought, hold it, don't bother to look for his photograph, you've seen it before, with the small, hard nose and the thoroughly-oiled hair, you know that face, and the narrow face with the fluffy hair which McAllen destroyed in the haystack. I left the page to flap, sat down and stroked my head with my hands. I was with the dead again, my old mates the dead. In Korea I buried dead bodies; I never use the word corpse to myself. That word corpse has the hollow, useless sound of garbage, as if a man were a walnut, a hard-shelled creation to be consumed either by cracking or else by a white worm which burns its round tunnel through the shell, devours the kernel

32

and leaves the inner walls black as if from burning. One day they machine-gunned us in the field where we were burying all the dead people. Afterwards we had to bury two of our own party. It was a change, to handle such fresh bodies. We used a lot of brandy.

With my finger-nail I traced the grain of the library table. Perhaps I could explain my madness. I knew it was only, so far, a minor madness, a wild cat, not a tiger. It was explicable, like the dark. I could even get fond of it like an old cat, an old wound. Not like some of the dirty madnesses you meet, the dirty ones with fetishes and writing on the walls. A rather special madness, elephantiasis of the conscience, the hatred of killing. A madness with a difference. The only madness that contains new formula Pitti. You can die of it. But there are no fetishes, no writing on the wall. I recalled writing on a cursorily whitewashed wall. The night was freezing, so full of mist that I felt I was standing on the floor of the North Sea. So I drew an arrow pointing to heaven and wrote: 'Are you bastards trying to freeze us off this planet?'

One past night was clear in my head, a few nights after my leg was hit. I lay thinking in that hospital, while the breathers and coughers around me rose into painful consciousness and fell back again, adding together all my beliefs. They weighed nothing. Religion meant Christ, ignored or misinterpreted by everyone. A good dead man whose name was shouted on battlefields. I knew little about science except for Heisenberg's Uncertainty Principle, which I had written on the fly-leaf of an introverted little novel called *Smoker's Cough*. I had written: 'If you can tell where an electron is, you cannot tell where it is going; and if you can tell where it is going, you can't tell where it is.' I was uncertain if I had written it down accurately. Had Heisenberg, whom I pictured more as a university than a man, said this sorrowfully or with a sneer? I was even ignorant about death, which I had seen happening. Death might be a paralysing drug, which cemented down all the outer signs of life, suspended the heart and lungs while the

33

senses and mind raced on, a paralysis which set in at a high point of pain, beyond which incommunicable pain climbed on, reaching its peak in the agony of decomposition.

I remembered fingering the cold metal rail of the hospital bed as I thought of people laughing. Joe particularly, a laughter addict. But when I thought of his laughter, which could rock a street like a canoe, the picture of him came to me on a silent film, and I could only see the mechanics of his mouth as it stretched, twisted slightly, opened wide, jerked and folded, opened again suddenly, drawing thin lines of shadow at the corners of his eyes and under them, closed in spasms, tensed and then calmed. Then I remembered the notice I saw in the director's waiting-room of a car factory: 'Men are valuable just in proportion as they are able and willing to work in harmony with other men.' Joe and I were both in Korea, but he was dead, no longer willing, able or valuable. I lay back watching the atoms of darkness spinning through the ward, the buzz of the hot evening or my head in the background, and recited that notice over and over, probably aloud. The joke of it returned to me, the kind of joke that makes you clench your muscles as you laugh. My throat joyfully began sending out laughter again. Somebody threw a boot and somebody else laughed himself into mild hysteria, but things began to improve for a while.

I left the Library. The branch had been removed, probably the Council had a place for old branches. People walked quickly by me, their feet banging the morning pavements because of all the small tensions making them hurry, and with each impact of leather on stone I saw the line at the side of each well-fed face, the line from the side of the nostril to the edge of the mouth, flicker and go out and flicker again. Above them the buses lurked like blue elephants. I passed a window full of metal desks, all empty, a window full of untouched document forms, a window full of gold rings. I remembered that I must sit down at a desk and write a will, that I must get married some day; I remembered isolated days of happiness when

I had more money than I needed. I remembered that this was such a day, and with wonder in my mind I let my fingers stray through the 137 pound notes in my pocket. The street looked prettier. I decided to collect my bag from the theatre and move into my room.

Insolently parked outside the theatre was an American Ford as long as the theatre. Inside the Ford, lounging among smoky air, was my brother. Coincidentally he is called Ford. My mother died before he started talking and my father named him Ford because he said all babies looked alike. Ford and I have both lived much of our lives in the States and most of our lives apart. I hadn't seen him for a year. He swung open the door and nodded to me. I moved in beside him.

'Hi, Johnny.' I laughed. We had nothing in common except a mother and father, American accents and a taste for whisky.

'What are you doing these days, Ford?'

'A ball,' he said, pulling out bourbon from the glove compartment for me. 'I'm a cleaner. I clean the base at North Shirleigh. Yanks and money go together.'

He looked rich, especially for a cleaner. He is browner, bigger and younger than me. He stayed on in the States till 1956, I came back to England when I retired from the Korean war. As far as I knew, my father was still playing Englishmen with large chins for Hollywood.

'Are the rackets good?'

He gave me a mock frown together with a half-smile.

'The world is beautiful. Each month a Yank can get five bottles of the stuff for eight bob a time, 40-ounce bottles, or gin for six and six. I'm in and out of the base all day. Evenings I sing rock with the station band. Good money, good money.'

'But Shirleigh's thirty miles away. Why come to Belston?'

'I can't sell the stuff too near the source. Anyway, Joan told me you were here.'

'You came to look for me?'

'Pass the time of day, man, maybe some drinking. I'm

making good money. One day soon I'll get back Stateside. Get a singing job.'

My father sang all over the States before he decayed into a screen butler. I sing, Ford sings, only Joan doesn't sing. Soon Ford and I were in the Unicorn, alternating lager and scotch, singing gently now and then.

'America, America,' said Ford. 'I can't wait. Maybe I'm English-born but I don't dig the blokes too much. Gang of ice cubes.'

'You're wrong,' I told him. 'The English are very warm, look how they treat the blind. The blind are given white sticks so that everyone will be kind to them. And given dogs to do their seeing for them, and basket-weaving as a career, and pity. The English know how to treat everyone, the deaf and dumb, the manic depressive, the American, the child, the Jew, the cripple, the unemployed, the Negro, the Youth, the Russian—and all because we have an unwritten tradition of treating everyone differently according to his deserts.'

I broke into one of Ben's songs:

> 'Rich man in his castle,
> Poor man at the gate,
> The suffering man
> Is the man I hate.'

'Your voice gets better,' said Ford.

'Why don't you take voice lessons?'

Ford laughed. 'Oh, Johnny, classes. What do they do? They cultivate you, man, they cultivate you. Here comes a virgin voice, professor. Oh fine, let's cultivate it. Take the Adam's apple out of his throat, let's have a look, tch, tch, too bad. Spanner please, haveta replace a cylinder here, drop of oil. Close the lid, how does it go? Still knocking? Hell, man, that's no sort of voice. I'm a goddam fool, I left the spanner in. That's better. I hereby decree that this Ford has a souped-up voice and can sing like Dame Patti Melba.

'So I look for an ad says New Dame Patti Melba Wanted for Rock Combo. Nothing today. Nothing tomorrow. Maybe not, says the professor, but his voice is sharp, ooh, sharp as a knife, did I tell you I carry a knife, Johnny?— yeah, that pocket. Well, you read the papers. Some guy gets jumped every day. Every damn day, every damn night some guy gets jumped. Comes to everyone. Big laugh when they jump me. Here comes trouble, Ford. Here comes Ford, trouble. And the trouble for trouble is that Ford got a knife. I do all right, I sing all the time, I know all the blues, I got a good job, nobody minds if I sing. Sing all over the place, nobody gives a damn. Except sometimes they say close down, you bastard. Witty bunch of chaps up at the campus.'

'Why not sing in England? My agent could help.'

'Show business in England? It makes the angels laugh. My friends are in the States, they're trying to get me a good manager now. I need a manager, see, someone with ideas. Only idea I ever had for show business was one night watching TV with a girl, she was a button-sewer in New Jersey. Petting around from the right angles I managed to watch the screen on and off for three hours. Thing struck me. All the girls on TV were about seventy-seven per cent better than the girl I was with. All the girls on TV are lookers.

'I started to feel sorry for all those plain girls who looked all right but never got on TV, and then I felt sorry for all the plain ugly girls who'd never see a camera. So I thought maybe they should take a Tuesday afternoon—not a Saturday night or anything like that—every week and run an hour called The Ugly Show, for ugly people to come on and talk and do acts. Give them a chance. Then I thought no, nobody thinks they're ugly except people who wouldn't want to be on TV because they got bad spots or something. So you'd have no show, unless you went round taking secret films of ugly people. Maybe that would make some of the ugly people feel better because they'd see people uglier than themselves. Then I began to get sorry for this button-sewing chick, well, she wasn't ugly, but she qualified for the Plain Square Show.'

'You can't do anything,' I said. 'But it bothers me too. Even pretty girls ugly themselves. I was on this bus in London and the girl in front of me had one of those round baskets. There was a furry toy monkey hanging from the handle on a piece of thread. The fur on the monkey's head was all round a little pale plastic face with white lips. That girl was stroking the monkey for all the way on the bus, she was about seventeen. When she got up I saw that her own hair, it was short but very thick and furry, was all clustered round her cheeks, leaving a little space for her face. And she was wearing white lipstick—'

'But those ugly girls,' said Ford. 'They do bother me. Most chicks are all right. I can sit in the car and give marks from one to five to the kids I dig as they walk on past. An ordinary chick gets one point if she's lucky. I can get two points out of almost any old bus queue. But what hits me from time to time is the real ugly ones. Some of them are so bad you can't look twice, and you feel bad yourself for feeling that way. And then you see one of these shiny chicks, four points at least.'

'Ford, you are a sad and serious boy.'

'I sleep very well.'

'This scotch is sending me to sleep, I better be moving.'

'Yeah, I better be back at base. I'll be in later this week, see you then. Oh, but Johnny, did you hear Ben Lewis is around?'

'At the International. I read it this morning.'

'I saw him. He's playing at the jazz club tonight. International's shut on Mondays.'

'I'll drop round. Will you be there?'

'No chance. There's this ugly chick . . .'

Big brown Ford swayed into his big blue Ford and sailed away up the street and out of sight. I obstructed the pavement while I tried to work out why Ford wanted to see me. We liked each other, but Ford likes plenty of people.

I collected my leather bag from the Acorn and walked to my room.

Mrs Rogers, my landlady, was exactly as I remembered her, small, warm and dominating, with a rugged chin, the cook of the biggest breakfasts in the Commonwealth. You had to keep old envelopes for the thick chunks of liver which came with two eggs, two bacon rashers, two pieces of fried bread and two cups of coffee or three of tea, not to mention grapefruit, Soggo, toast, and bread and butter. The envelopes were posted down the lavatory.

'You need some sleep,' she told me.

'I know it. I'm just going to get some, Mrs Rogers.'

My room was completely square, a box lined long ago with flowered paper. I could not identify those brown and maroon blossoms. As the afternoon town was wide open to the August sun, my window was also wide open. Below I could see Bill Rogers, his ancient aggressive face peering over the handlebars of his tricycle at a sandy boy of six or seven. Bill is my landlady's eight-year-old son, the tricycle was too young for him, but he used the saddle like a king's throne. In a clear, cunning voice he addressed the other boy:

'What can you see?'

'Where?'

'In the street, in the street.'

'There's cars, and—um—some people.'

'Anything else?'

'Houses?'

'Of course there are houses. Anything else?'

'Don't think so. Yes, a bike. And you, Bill.'

There was a long pause, then Bill said: 'Can you see God?'

'No, I can't see him.'

Bill pointed up the street. 'You're not looking,' he said. 'Who's that walking there?'

'Can't see anyone.'

Bill moved his tricycle forward so that its front wheel pushed against the boy's hip. The boy moved back one step. Bill shoved him with his hand.

39

'You're a pagan, you're not trying to see God.'

'I am, I am, I can't see him.'

'There he is, can't you see him? There he is.'

Bill hit the boy, who stood as if he deserved it, but bewildered, staring round him.

'Yes, I can see him now. I can.'

Bill relaxed. 'What does he look like?'

'What do you mean?'

'What does he look like?'

'He's big.'

'What colour is God?'

'A sort of dark colour. He's big.'

'What sort of dark colour?'

'Just dark.'

'What about Jesus? Is Jesus with him?'

'I'm not sure.'

'There, look over there, just in front of God.'

'Oh yes, Jesus is there.'

'What's he like?'

'Bill he's—he's got a beard.'

'All right. Is he a light colour?'

'Yes, a light colour.'

'What sort of light colour?'

'A kind of gold I think.'

'You're getting better. Has he got a crown on his head?'

'Yes'.

'What sort of crown?'

'It's a crown. Is it a sort of gold? I don't know.'

Bill moved his tricycle forward again.

'You're a little liar,' he said. 'You can't see God or Jesus at all. I think I ought to hit you.'

I put my head out of the window. I said: 'Leave him alone,' and the smaller boy ran away. Bill watched him, not me, and almost immediately Mrs Rogers looked out of her front room.

'Leave him alone,' she shouted, but she was looking up at me, not down at Bill. She had to twist her head round to see me and that twisted her face in an uncanny way,

40

so I pulled in my head quickly. Perhaps Bill could see God and Jesus. I looked out again. I couldn't see God or Jesus, but I could see Mrs Rogers.

I closed the window to keep out the combined noises of one hundred streets. My sense of hearing has always amazed me, not only because of its power to detect unpleasantness at a distance, the approaching cop or the six-ton lorry, the avenging female or the comradely male, but also because of its various prejudices. It is pleased by raucous voices, the tearing of cardboard, the minor thunder of a fast typewriter, the slamming of heavy doors, the pouring of drinks. The anticipation of breaking glass or china stretches my eardrums taut with excitement. My ears object to the sounds of silk, eating, and string instruments under the bow. So if I am fastidious in anything, it is in the noises which I choose when there is any choice.

Silence, that ideal noise, cannot be reached. At times I have imagined it attainable, have gone to my room and sealed the door with underwear, drawn the blind and heavy curtains on a closed window and lain on the bed, ears plugged with the cotton-wool from old aspirin bottles. After a short period of warm buzzing, the settling of old springs in the bed under my ear, other noises begin. I hear the workings of my body and limbs and head, the blood walking up and down the arteries, and my heart takes up its mallet in an effort to break out of my chest. Soon all the traffic of the streets is diverted between my left and right ears. I've tried this trick four times, and always I end up laughing, an absurd ostrich in a rowdy desert.

I carried this experiment further once, more or less beyond laughter, because one of the men I remembered best in the hospital was not only blind and deaf, but quietly mad. It was only a matter of time, they said. He could talk, so they could tell he was mad, very rigid formal sentences, nearly always categorical statements, usually untrue. That time I bandaged my eyes and stuffed my ears, not purely from curiosity: I wanted to understand the man. I didn't try to simulate his madness as well, I had a

41

small one of my own. The experiment lasted about ten minutes. Don't try it. Once this sort of experiment fascinated me, but I realized that to try to cut off one or two senses temporarily is destructive and distorting. Using all the senses at the same time is more inspiring. Use all five at once and you're almost flying, use all your muscles as well and you are making love, you are the Archangel Gabriel in a bed of rainbows. I wiped my face on the clean pillow. Velma and I were similar but not the same. Though her hands were all about me during the clothed part of the day, when we made love they were still, resting hands. Her body accepted but did not give.

Calm again, I loosened my collar and imagined myself eating a spoonful of honey. It was like eating clean, rough sunlight. There were lines all over my hands, meaning nothing or simply illegible. I struck a match. It burned like a thin poet. My mind was playing tricks on me again, showing me pretty pictures. But it calmed me; like a child, I needed pretty pictures before sleep, and spoonfuls of honey. I required the company of dogs.

I thought of steep Seattle. I lived there with one of my dead mother's sisters while Ford stayed in Chicago for the war. My aunt was wide and breezy as Seattle itself, I could sleep in the house if I wanted or under the piers or in a canoe. She was funniest when she was drunk on German beer, but she loved me best when she was sober. At school I was happy; it was run on the gang system. There were several fighting gangs, all the gangs fought, but there was no other reason for the fighting gangs. They would give their black eyes to be in a fight, shoulder anyone out of the way, swear at anyone, especially a Jap. Some fighting gangs carried an intellectual. He survived by using a violent and damaging tongue, by hurling long festoons of abuse round an enemy, by the blackmailer's file he kept in his memory.

There was a baseball gang, of course, and a football gang which was really one of the bigger fighting gangs. The

42

fishing gang was never very well integrated. Those fishers were respected, however, because they were hairier than anyone else and always carried fish-hooks. I was in the singing gang, one of the smallest, but all of us toughly dedicated, willing to fight for our music. Good voices all round, stubbornly in unison between classes, before and after school; in the vacations and in the evenings you could hear us plodding through the songs of the day. Then, one autumn, a tall young Negro called Joe Kelly came to take charge of us. He came from Kansas City, his father was a band singer, and Joe made us work. As we sweated to learn harmony and the simple, swinging arrangements he invented and copied for us, we were entirely happy, we had found our master. Joe played boogie piano, and his mother let us sing till our throats burnt in her front room. She brought us tall glasses of iced water on a green tray. The other gangs began to listen to our vibratos, we were booked for parties. Joe added a drummer to his piano, then a trumpet. He taught us the blues, Kansas City style, and we learned to sneer when asked for a hit tune. Joe would sit among us, tall back curved, fingers hammering the keys, his almost circular head held low as our cool voices swarmed around his deep, driving voice. We watched Joe, never the audience, and he would grin as we all travelled together. I never saw Joe in Korea, but he died in that war. His mother told me he died quickly. Falling asleep, I remembered Joe as he used to sing:

'If you see me comin', sash your window high,
  Now if you see me comin', sash your window high,
  And if you see me goin', hang your head and cry.'

I slept until the afternoon began to cool. Downstairs Mrs Rogers called me into her sitting-room, a frequent privilege in the old days. I had lapped some scotch from a plastic mug before going down, it brought back good times and good feelings. I liked Mrs Rogers but not Bill, who

43

sat stolidly with big eyes in front of the TV set. Nor did I like the Rogers cat, which often jumped on me from the dark heights of my wardrobe. The cat was in a domestic mood, it was looking for somewhere to rest its untired body, I could guess what it was going to do. Inevitably the room contains one small mat. I was tense, awaiting the preordained platitude of an attitude. It would be unlucky for me if it happened. It happened. On a black mat, a mat as black as a black cat, the cat, as smooth as a smooth mat sat, as black as a black mat, on a mat as smooth as a smooth black cat. The cat sat on the mat.

In the corner the moulded wood TV set, a sawn-off cyclops with a swelling pink plastic lens over the screen, showed me a man talking to a giraffe.

'So we call him Measles,' said the man. 'Incidentally, do you know why the giraffe is so tall? It's so he can reach those lovely succulent leaves at the top of the tree.' He took a sudden little step backwards as the giraffe lowered its pinhead. 'But now let's go and see what the monkeys are up to.'

A deeply weary voice took over as another camera showed a gorgonzola sculpted in cement, in and out of the holes of which fell, climbed and jumped hairy cheesemites.

'Monkey Palace,' said the voice, 'was presented to the Zoo in 1928 by Lord Tartar. Lord Tarter himself often comes down to watch the jolly little fellows at play, and indeed this is one of the most popular attractions in the whole Zoo.'

About twenty of the monkeys were methodically beating up a smaller monkey half-way up the cheese palace, and it became a scene for Bosch as they scratched each other and fell out of sight. A knot of quieter monkeys in the semi-foreground were out of focus.

'Hello again,' said the first voice as the camera contemplated a rectangular rhinoceros and the rhinoceros contemplated back. 'Here we have a very funny fellow, the rhinoceros. Well, the rhino, as you can see, has a horn, and

44

a very dangerous weapon it looks to be sure, as you can see.'

The other voice broke in: 'These birds take their name of Lyre-birds from their delicately shaped tails, which are, as you can see, in the shape of lyres.'

But the picture had not changed, and there in the middle of its concrete plain the rhino was emptying the food and water of several days in a mock Niagara. The flood continued for half a minute, and then the famous backside of a Lyre bird came into view. It was shaped like a lyre.

'And with that,' said the voice of a girl up to her eyes in tranquillizers, 'we must conclude our visit to the Zoo— so back to the studio.'

In the half-length picture which followed she appeared to be wearing nothing but a script. I recognized her as Betty Tye, an actress who went through the men of the Acorn Theatre like a scythe through asparagus. I doubted if she was wearing anything except a script.

'And now,' said Betty, 'Personal Problem, a new series in which viewers' worries are mulled over by panellists James Devon and Margaret Rose Mercer.'

I switched off my eyes and left. James Devon, Personality, is my best enemy. I know him.

The butt of the afternoon I spent playing Ellington's 'Such Sweet Thunder' in the record section of Blooter's, the all-embracing store. I bought a paperback called *How High the Stars* by Jett B. Kampbell to read in the park. It was set in A.D. 3558 on Gurt X, the shaking planet. Most of the characters were sadistic, telepathic mutants, surgically manufactured freaks, or super-intelligent robots. The three factions were striving for domination. But from the slave-race of oppressed humans rose one man with a secret which could destroy the galaxy, Cain Douglas, descendant of a race of star-conquerors. I tried dutifully to identify myself with Douglas, but that meant I had to identify nearly everyone else as mutants, freaks and robots. Only James Devon clearly fitted each category. It was an ugly book, dirty with gratuitous pain, so I threw it away.

In Lyons I shovelled into my cement-mixer mouth two doughnuts, two buns smeared with wet butter, a cardboard sausage roll and a large coffee. I was drunk with the thought of singing with Ben's piano for my voice to walk on. Hours later I arrived at the jazz club, an inner glow of scotch and Old Jack Strong Ale in my stomach. Miles Davis, on record, was squeezing sour drops from his trumpet. Among the tables, sucking at a Coke, wandered Ben. He had trimmed his beard, his tie was hairy and orange. As soon as he saw me he laughed.

'How is it? How is it?'

'Great. How's the music?'

'They give me money for it these days, he boasted.'

'How's the women?'

'Intermittent, he opined.'

'Are you around for long?'

'About two months, he offered hesitantly.'

'I'm in this Acorn show. Singing vocal songs with words.'

'I know that, man—my little sister's in the show. Sheila. Haven't you heard her?'

'She's your sister? I heard her on Jazz Club. I knew she was on the bill and I knew she was good, but I didn't know she had far-out relations. And I didn't know you had relations at all.'

'Here she is, he apologized.'

Sheila was taller than Ben. Dark hair and a long mouth smiling, her black skirt with its single hoop of colours almost hid the spider-legged stool on which she sat, so that she appeared to be suspended only by the air she breathed so generously. Her blouse outside her skirt was white and covered with large, obsolete gold coins. She said nothing as she smiled, as she accepted a gulp from my half-bottle of scotch, as she looked round my face like a wife looking round a new house. I could feel the lines under my eyes telling her one story and the lines at the edges of my eyes telling her another, all the lines of my face being given the same attention, as if she were using some infinitely

46

delicate tracing paper on which to record my face. I couldn't mind, she was so gentle.

'Ben told me about you,' she said. 'He said you cut your finger-nails a lot.'

'Well, they grow fast, they're very brittle, you know—is that all he told you?'

'He said you can't play tennis.'

'I don't want to play tennis. I'd forgotten that I can't play tennis.'

Ben took my arm and Sheila's and walked us to the piano.

'Look at him,' I said. 'I've known him five years and all he knows about me is finger-nails and tennis.'

'He said you sing.'

'That was very big of him.'

'First I'll sing for you. Then you sing for me,' said Sheila, and waved for silence. The piano revved up. From Sheila came a voice, styled after Sarah Vaughan's, its phrasing complex, its range starting deeper than Sarah's and not rising to those snowy heights. She sang with her brown eyes open, aimed at a grubby corner of the ceiling sometimes, and sometimes, with a touch of amusement, at me. The voice was so cool and clever that I wanted to laugh and fall about. She sang one of Ben's bopped-up blues:

'Dig my grave long and shallow—eight by eight by three,
Dig my grave long and shallow—eight by eight by three,
Fill my pretty mouth with gelignite, ears full of T.N.T.

'Light the fuse, my baby, watch me flying through the air,
Light the fuse, retire, see me gliding through the air,
If I'm going to heaven, I'll have to be blown up there.

'Like a great big sponge that the sun's been shinin'
        through,
Just like a crazy sponge that the sun's been shinin'
        through,
Feel so damned empty I don't care what I do.

47

'Well, the sea beats a rock and it makes it smooth and
  round,
Yes the sea beats a rock and it makes it smooth and
  round,
And the smoother your lover, the longer he's been around.

'When that love rolls in, you can't make it turn about.
No when love rolls in, baby, you can't make it turn about.
And when the tide changes, you can't stop it running out.'

Singing made her talkative: 'Things happen to me,' she
said. 'New things happen all the time and you can't do
anything. I asked a man the way to the club. He didn't
know, so he told me everything he did know. He was on
the buses for forty years. They just put his rent up. He'd
spent ninety-five pounds on the house in the last two years
and the landlord wouldn't help. There was something
sinister about the drains. His son was in Australia. He told
me about Australia. He had me wait in the street while he
fetched his photograph album. So on and so on. The whole
business took half an hour.'

'Be careful,' said Ben.

'He was tame. He just wanted to talk. I want to talk.'

She went on talking, but it was half-nonsense talk, scat
speaking. She took a theme, stated it, then improvised
round it, while her voice, face and gestures all put spring
into her words. When she mouthed the word 'tiger' for
instance, in that quarter-second she implied a growl in her
voice, stretched out the fingers of her right hand as if she
wore claws, braced her upper lip as if for stiff tiger whiskers,
and leaned forward. There was no time for her to change
into stripes, for by this time she was changing herself into
the next operative word, maybe 'wardrobe', with a long
wooden face and a concealed echo chamber at the back
of her throat. Sometimes the variations were pleasingly
fantastic, sometimes they were sabre-toothed comments,
but always they come to a firm conclusion. Sheila can
make up her mind on anything.

'He had this moustache, all yellow,' she said. 'And after a while he started to pull it. He went on pulling it. Then he offered me five shillings. For talking to him. I settled for a cigarette. He had to fetch it from the house and he brought a table-lighter. It was as big as a dictionary.'

'I like matches better than lighters,' she said as she inhaled one of mine. 'Lighters are for mechanics. You get them after twenty-five years' service with the coffin company. Tories give them to each other. The wicks are made too large, because the makers know most people don't carry pliers, they can't pull the wicks up. They have to buy another lighter. The profit motive. The petrol goes all over the place and you catch fire. Floosh! Up goes everything and you're not insured and you burn down and all that's left is the lighter.'

'Sing, Johnny', said Ben. 'She's exhausted. She won't talk again for another two days.'

'I like talking to him,' said Sheila. 'But someone ought to sing.'

It was my turn. My feet were not too steady. We decided on a slow version of 'The Comeback'. I kept wetting my lips as Ben's piano rolled through the first chorus, fiddled with the mike, my hand sweaty and no use for adjusting anything, even a tie, if I had been wearing one. My hands fell to my hips as I put my feet apart for security and let out a loud oh-oh-ho on one high note, then swooped down to take the proud first verse:

'I know my baby is gonna jump and shout,
I know, I know my baby, she gonna jump and shout,
When the train rolls in and her Daddy come walkin' out.'

I had them all, their faces were pink oval lights beamed at me, and Sheila's eyes were big. I hit such a note, such a note suddenly, I held it, hating to leave it, letting it grow in front of my eyes like a balloon blowing up. That was a good note, a solid note that filled my whole body and then flew. I was leaning forward, some fault of posture

due to the bad habits of youth no doubt, and if you looked
at me objectively I was the Problem of the Youth of this
Country incarnate. My right foot was flipping against the
wooden platform, my fingers clicking at the end of my
arms, fingers which carry the offbeat subconsciously like
real live American fingers. Faces began to shout encour-
agement. I was shouting back. I ran out of verses, I remembered some more from another blues, we took it at double
tempo. I opened out my voice like a sports car, speeded so
happily. There was my baby, waiting for the train to pull in,
I hoped she was waiting:

'There, there goes my baby, run and call her back,
 There goes my baby, run and call her back,
 That girl carries something that I really like.'

There was a piano and drum explosion and we braked.
Sheila was stroking the back of her neck and smiling
widely, Ben was laughing. We decided on a duet, 'Baby,
It's Cold Outside' with bongos. As we sang, it stood out
like a volcano in a smokeless zone. Apart we were good,
together we were a machine for producing blue clouds,
black rain, a golden steamroller—the extra beauties that
children dream about even while they are possessed by
the loveliness of a piece of wire, a parade, their own bodies,
a mouse or box of matches. We were the invention of
bacon and eggs. We sang 'Can't We be Friends?', Sheila
sang Ben's words to 'Bernie's Tune', then I took Ben's
raucous 'When Tina Grinds the Coffee':

'When Tina grinds the coffee
 She grinds more than enough.
 When Tina grinds the coffee
 It's not that instant stuff.
 Now I'm a little boy just out of my teens
 But there ain't much left of my coffee beans,
 When Tina grinds the coffee
 Well it's not that instant stuff.'

50

We finished together with 'Let's Do It'. By this time all the whisky was taking roots and my head felt conical, like a paper hat with candy stripes in purple and shining white spiralling up it, while my hair in front was drying and the water I had smeared on it had evaporated. The forelock bounced into my eyes too often. Not only was my hair drying, but the alcohol, I felt sure, was drying my skin, the skin of my face felt dry to touch, though it was hot enough to sweat. I slumped into a chair while Sheila stood by her brother, ready to sing down the four winds with one mighty blues, her eyes looking down at her feet, her hands touching each other below her hypnotic breasts.

I have so many recurring picture thoughts in my head that sometimes my brain is beaten into a parade ground for old pictures. They form up, perform their intricate marching and counter-marching—landscapes, furniture, faces alive and faces dead. But when there is a new picture of importance, the worn square of my thoughts is cleared. And there was tall Sheila, still, watching her feet while her mouth shifted and distorted and trouble poured from her lips. It was a puny, weary, remembering song. The words said it was a song about a girl so bored she took to heroin, then got bored with the habit itself. But the way Sheila sang it it sounded like a song about love:

'I got used to the jab,
I got used to the jolt,
I got used to the shiver
And the thunderbolt,
What's the use, honey?
You get used to it all.

'Got used to the visions
And the sense of sin,
I got used to the little marks
All over my skin.
What's the use, baby?
You get used to it all.'

She began like that. By the end she had dispensed with words, she hummed, spoke and corncraked tatters of the blues. The soiled, blasé little song had turned the deepest shade of blue. Her sweet wide mouth closed, she stood watching her feet. I realized she had stopped singing. I took her hand and said she was beautiful. But I was sick with the excitement of my new picture and I had to get back to my room.

TUESDAY

THAT WAS A BAD NIGHT. I had expected to sleep quietly under that load of scotch, with that picture of Sheila and the musical sounds of her to soothe me. But my head was lined with stone, it was occupied by the prison I had never seen.

The clock was pacing quickly in the direction of the hanging. The prison was riotous with thoughts and voices.

The prisoners: By Christ there he goes. Listen. No, make a bloody row. There he goes, the poor bugger. Hit the bars, bash the bloody ground.

The padre: Our Father which art I'm not going to look but I'll touch him on the arm just like this, just his arm, just the sleeve round his arm, I wish he'd walk more quickly hallowed be Thy name.

The governor: I'm not going through it again. The bastard. I'm not going to do it again. Count. Thirty-seven, thirty-eight, thirty-nine, fifty no forty, forty-one, forty-two, forty-three.

The hangman: A black shape is in his head. His thoughts come under the Official Secrets Act. He stands, moves, officially, with more authority than anyone. Through the conscience of millions who gave him that authority, a small pale conscience, a near-dead organ which could drop off through disuse, a few twitches pass.

McAllen is saying his thoughts out loud: Christ, he says with every outward breath, Christ, Christ, Christ, Christ.

53

The rope goes heavily round his neck, it is so heavy they have to hold him standing. Christ, Christ, the word comes louder and then weaker as the man's mind circles the prison like a motor-cyclist over the cinders. Through the dust he can only shout the possible countersign to death—Christ—but he is so dry in the mouth that only those standing within touch but outside his reach can hear the word before it drops. Christ with every breath, but Christ does not join the small terrified group.

The clock, set back, paced in the direction of the hanging. The prison was riotous with thoughts and voices. I couldn't tell when I was asleep, when I was awake. It was only Tuesday. McAllen was still waiting, he wouldn't be over until Saturday morning. I was all sweat. I turned over to face a new scene.

The independent commission sent by the Tory Government in Rome had submitted a lop-sided report on the Calvary incident. Even so, it was generally agreed that there had been some mistake in the colony, inevitable, even tragic. But think of all the Jews who were not crucified by mistake. Millions. Thousands, anyway.

The Minister for the Colonies spoke with quiet pride of his faith in the man on the spot, Pontius Pilate. If the execution was unfortunate, everything had been done to ensure that this did not happen again. As a first move towards better relations, Barabbas had been crucified as well.

The Labour Opposition was uneasy. Said the Shadow Colonial Minister: 'This is not enough to underline the good faith of Rome towards her people. Under a Labour government rehabilitation measures would have been carried even further. Those two corporals would have lost their stripes for dicing on duty.'

Them and their bloody bomb. The old monks said that a female bear gave birth to shapeless lumps, which she then licked into shape with her tongue, sculpting her young in her own image. There are big-tongued statesmen about who would like to lick us all out of shape, lick us until we are a formless semi-liquid, easily controlled and channelled. The mass may flow contentedly in peacetime. When a war approaches, the big men just light a bunsen burner under the flow, and the stuff begins to bubble and steam, there is plenty of functional hatred. The people I dig are the people who refuse to be licked. I felt as if I had been licked all over by a hot tongue.

Stripped of my fur, lowering myself on hands and knees into the stinging hotness of bath water, I acclimatized each successive inch of nerve-webbed skin. Small wet clouds climbed past my head. There was a mirror and I saw myself. On all fours, a tired wild animal, wondering which species it belonged to.

With one finger I wrote 'Neurotic' on the steamed paint of the wall. I underlined it. Then I put it in brackets because I am one of the secret neurotics. We hide. We avoid doctors. We slyly recognize each other by signs, like Masons and Ovaltinies. We even hide the terrible armed thoughts from ourselves by reading, talking, working, singing, drinking and loving too much. We disguise our animal natures by noting conventional standards of decency and secrecy, and then aping them. We try, grant us that, we try to be good, even though we are ruling the minds of apes with the wills of infants. Forgive us, though you may not recognize us in our disguises. If you can forgive us our occasional berserk nights, maybe we can learn to understand the killing habits of civilization, even to accept them when we are very, very old. Well, all right then.

I slept until noon, despite Mrs Rogers. Then I spent a long time shaving the dark stubble which grew so oddly below my white hair. It was time to revisit the Unicorn. In the long bar I saw the man I hated most in the world, but Velma was in his group so I took my Guinness and sat down violently beside, deliberately not opposite, TV's Uncle James Devon in the flesh. He haunts Belston because his famous farm is two miles outside the town. At the same time I managed to sit opposite Velma, the simultaneous achievements of the one action pleasing me. From here I would not have to watch the soft Cotswold face of Devon, or be incited to throw good stout in his face, or answer directly, looking into those narrow eyes, his police-man questions, or notice when his glass emptied or his pipe died, or be in a position to overturn the table on top of him or to suddenly produce a ten-foot banner embroidered with 'The Hell With You and Your Dishonest Mouth.' For I am given to ill-considered and fierce manifestoes on any subject you care to name, while Devon replies with a face of placid sorrow as if he hoped to die a virgin saint. This forty-five-year-old Union Jack, farthest flung of our imperial outposts, is so awash with unenlightened self-interest that he destroys my tennis-lawn temper like some giant mole. He once said into my ear: 'I am England, and so, my friend, are you.'

Sometimes Devon broadcasts on country matters in an assumed accent. On TV he will sit beside a scale model of the latest village he has conquered and point to a building.

'So I went to see dear old Mrs Monkworth . . .'

We fade in on Mrs Monkworth, who is fading out, and there is fat Devon chewing her home-made cakes and asking about her husband.

'I believe he passed away at Arnhem,' murmers Devon with some awe.

'I bloody well did not,' says an off-screen voice, in my day-dreams. After one of these rural tours, Devon is driven out of the countryside by Elsa, his large secretary, not by the enraged inhabitants, to a hotel suite in London or to the Belston flat from which he likes to survey his farm. But in all the money splendour of his money rooms, decor-ated in the eighteenth-century money style, where he can relax for a few money hours with money, Devon has never lost the common touch, which means he bothers poor sods like me. He knew my father well, and he says he enjoys the conversation of young people.

Devon knew me as a child, and treats me now as Aunt Deborah treated me when I was six. (Aunt Deborah, little and silly, was called Your Poor Aunt Deborah by

Devon, perhaps because she was poor. She was the one who continually recounted the story about my rushing down the stairs after seeing the new window-cleaner with his beard, and shouting 'God's climbing in my room.' My objection to this story was not so much that she died repeating it, but that she insisted I was psychic, mainly because the window-cleaner was run over within a month of my remark.)

Now Devon was the centre of an unlikely group of five —Velma, Roger and the Markham twins sitting over glasses of lager, handling their cigarette-holders with an air of controlled insanity. One twin is male and the other is not. He is Simon, a pale tragic actor of comedy with a heart of lard, he would be in *Swing Low*. She is Deirdre, not so bad, a mean nurse at the local hospital. Roger, the superior antidote to Devon, was enjoying a joke with himself, blinking and grinning into his pint. As Simon paraded ideas, his sharp voice jabbed out through the fake burr of Devon, neither giving way, both in mid-sentence. Simon's punctuation was jerky and frequent. Devon rolled his head and burrowed onwards in his bowelly, official hum. Their rhythms were complicated by the introduction of Deirdre Markham's soprano, complaining about something, and the alto of Velma offering round cigarettes. The arrangement of voices was unappealing, but Roger acted as a rhythm section, thudding out platitudes between the bitter nothings of Simon and the rhetorical grumble of Devon. I became spellbound by Roger's rhythmic sense of conversation, he was hitting the off-beat with 'Prove it,' 'Have you *read* the book?', and 'How do you mean, socialist?', driving the soloists higher and higher with quiet phrases. With each squealed or bellowed solo the nonsense grew hotter, it became a cartoon parody of debate. I was busy coping with Velma's right foot, which was being friendly, and noticing that her left arm was round Roger's neck. The noise around me had lost all meaning. Then the voice of Devon, suddenly inflamed, rose above the talk:

'Of course if ever anybody deserved hanging, it was that fiend McAllen.'

I was shaking and I went out without looking at anyone, not wanting even to talk to Velma, who understood a percentage of my feelings. Maybe her heart would feel the cold in that man too, I thought, as I stood outside trying to light a cigarette. My fingers were clumsy. My mouth was still wet with stout, its lips would not stay still, so the cigarette tip fell apart and the sour tobacco crumbs stuck to my tongue. I wanted to lie down. Out of the bar came Velma. She walked in my direction, but for me it was my own direction, for me to travel alone. There was every reason not to stop for her, I wanted to lie down alone. Sutton Street, black with traffic, lay ahead; I turned down it, past a line of dark blue schoolgirls led by a solemn blonde. I would have run, trying to lose Velma, but I didn't want to make her run too, she was wearing crazy shoes and she might break her ankle. My leg might fail me, it was aching slightly, but I increased my stride and gathered momentum, turning round to see a hobbling Velma. Some way behind her was a streak of grey which might be Roger. I was gaining as I dodged into the gilded doorway of Blooter's, the department store, past the green statue of Charles Blooter.

Many shops are old-fashioned, but Blooter's is a historic monument. An employee once told me that when the slave trade was swinging, three six-foot slaves were chained in the main window marked 'This Season's Snip', 'Labour-Saving at its Best', and 'Guaranteed for Five Years'. I walked to the basement of the building—canvas chairs for the garden, stone gnomes for the loggia, then took a lift to Mattresses, where I saw Roger and Velma with their backs to me, hand in hairy hand. I waited behind a pillar, then slipped through Hardware, a mass of flashing pots and pans, a counter devoted entirely to knives. Sauntering among the lines of erect tents and green canoes, I formed my plan. The chase had cleared my mind of the encircling gloom; now it was a game. A salesman, hefty and blazered,

58

waited for action, transferring his centre of gravity from one foot to the other and patting the back of one hand into the palm of the other, noiselessly of course. I carefully planted one foot nine inches from the other, let it take root, held hands with myself behind my back, and assumed the face of a naval captain who has failed to go down with his ship.

The salesman shuffled brusquely and began: 'Can I get you anything, sir?'

'No . . . I don't think so, man.' I spoke slowly, trying not to focus my eyes, implying that I was past hope.

'Just like to look round? That's all right, sir.'

'No, I need a . . . like some—'

'What would it be, sir?'

'Underwater, y'know, like this Cousteau bit . . .'

'I understand. But what would you like?'

'For sharks, man.'

'Shark repellent powder perhaps, sir, for tropical sub-aquatics?'

'No, man, shark food.'

Letting my right knee sag, I clutched at an underwater harpoon with my left hand, dragging it from the plaster grip of a dummy sportsman. I fingered the trigger and collapsed realistically into a rubber boat marked 'Excelsior'. There I lay happily, eyes shut, hand fixed to the harpoon in sham rigor mortis.

'Are you all right, sir?'

I lay there. After a few questions and free brandy they let me lie down in their sick-room for two hours. That was all I wanted from Blooter's, except maybe some shark repellent powder for Devon.

I headed for the Museum because I felt like looking at monster bones; they usually cheered me up and they might take my mind off flesh; I was thinking too much about Sheila, who had walked without apologies into my mind as I lay on that hard Blooter bed.

After one century of grey rain under Belston Cliffs, Belston Municipal Museum looked as if it had been carved out of solid phlegm. Its floors are slippery as ice, with puddles of polish where it had been laid on too thickly to be absorbed by the already polish-sodden wood. I patted the bottle in my pocket. I had been mildly high for twenty-four hours and was only mildly worried about it. I walked through a hall of arms. All over the walls were geometrical patterns, like great metallic snowflakes, formed by daggers, swords, claymores, dirks, spears, blades for stabbing, slashing and disembowelling. A rest home of old killers. Each blade was polished and sharp. In the centre of the room was a marble block with a metal grille the size of a large waffle let into each side. It seemed too monumental for central heating, too well-aerated for a tomb. Its colour was a violent pink with long streaks of grey like the dark skin of a fish, and its edges were exactly cut. Three feet high and four feet square, it had mass but no meaning. It made a cold bench. I crouched beside it, but could see nothing except a faint light through the grilles.

The square-shaped attendant standing at ease in the far corner of the hall was watching me. I straightened and strolled, half-closing my eyes in an attempt to turn the circles, diamonds and squares of weapons into the snowflake patterns I had seen at first. Some success, but my eyes kept returning to that marble box. By fixing the position of windows, I worked out its latitude and longitude, I had to get inside that box; it might be a mushroom farm, an underground match factory or the place where the man sits contemplating a red button and waiting for the order to press it. After some exploration I found a dusty door, behind it were stairs leading downwards, unswept stone steps with old filter tips in the crevices. The door at the bottom had no handle, no lock, no bolts; it swung open, almost weightless, cheap wood nailed together. I could have made a better door.

I was in a stone corridor lit only by a small and dirty window, but that was lighting enough; it showed me where I was and where the marble box must be, A side door in the corridor led to a solid oak door with yellow finger plates, which led to two more doors. I had to hold open the third door to allow room for the fourth to open. It was a large rectangular lavatory with no windows, one seat and a pile of crackling newspapers. One low-powered bulb shone. I pushed all the bolts home and looked at the high ceiling. In the centre, almost directly above the seat and its cistern, was a square space, about four feet square, the hollow interior of the marble box.

I was alone again. As I sat down I instinctively drew the imaginary pistol from my hip and aimed it at the door. The door was ahead of me but three feet to my left. I would make a difficult target. They would have to drop a smoke bomb through the grilles above. I wished I had brought some food, it was a good place for a siege. I had some scotch instead.

Standing on the split wooden seat, I reached up and grabbed the edge of the cistern, and began to climb up the wall. It was made of that hard plaster which feels like smooth stone, and my feet walked over old inscriptions, inefficiently blurred by the museum staff. One writer boasted: 'I am the only intelligent man in Belston.' A Hellenist had left a long sprawl of Greek. Below, another hand had commented: 'I'm a tit man myself.' A complicated list about two feet by one foot listed the members of a household, together with their offences against the writer and their punishments. The chambermaid, Lizette, came off worst. I got my knee on the cistern, then my left foot, then slowly stood up. My leg hurt a little, but I could still climb on to a cistern. From my waist down I was still in the basement lavatory. My chest, neck and head were in the marble box.

Through one grille I could see dark blue trousers passing, probably the attendant. Behind him two good female legs and lines of little pegs in white socks. More children's legs, until the box was surrounded by them. Trying to turn round, I stepped on the cistern's lever, it plunged, and the lavatory flushed mightily. The noise roared up through my box, which acted as a loudspeaker, and the

61

silent children suddenly turned into laughers. They laughed so energetically for so long that they might have been paid to do it. It was a good sound. I would have paid to hear it.

I slipped down to the floor as the laughter vanished down the armoury. I half lay, making myself a comfortable nest of dead newspapers. I knew why the Museum was kept alive by circulating groups of postcard buyers. They came to see and touch the Heart of Belston. The Heart is an enormous rock of Belston stone, about the size of a double-decker bus, roughly shaped like a conventional heart, a Valentine to send to a statue. It is loved and treasured, it is the reason why the Museum stands immediately below the cliffs. Early in the Napoleonic wars the Heart had fallen from the heights and crushed a tall man with a rough voice and thick hair. He was a French saddler, suspected of being a spy. The Museum was built around the ragged rock, which features heavily in guide books, and there is a stone pub with bulging wall-paper and good beer named after it. The basement was hot. I began to sleep and dream.

I was lying in the Heart, and through its sides I could see a party of schoolchildren, because the rock had become transparent. It was a holiday as the children waited to climb on a bus at the top of the winding road down from the cliffs to the town. At first I couldn't see the bus driver, but as the rock around me rolled slowly closer I saw he was a very small man, like a dwarf version of Devon, being led through the crowd towards his seat. Several speeches were being made simultaneously by golden men. a band blared, and a few people were hanging and being hanged in the background. The dwarf, his face a round instrument indicating only happiness, was jerked into the air and carried into the driving seat of the bus. Postcards were being handed to me to send to everyone I knew, their jokes in the ancient seaside tradition, but these cards pictured not bulbous bathers but men and women with their bones jutting out of yellow skins. The children were all in the bus, and it became clear that although the bus driver was happy to the point of hysteria, he was also blind. Blind as a rock. The snow was grey, each flake equipped with spikes. It was falling inside my head, hurting my brain. A group of women in hats kept hanging the same man. The bus started down the cliff road and I was collecting tickets as Joe appeared at my side, mouthing words I could not hear. I woke cold, my head was dizzy and I needed a smoke. More than that, I needed air.

Climbing on to the cistern was more difficult this time. Another party was coming into the hall, a noisy group of adults. Those in the distance I could see full-length, they wore hats and cameras, they walked in line, perhaps they had influence. So I shouted through my marble loud-speaker into the chatting hall:

'Reprieve McAllen. Reprieve McAllen now. McAllen must not hang.'

They had to be slogans. I had not the scope to explain my reasons, let alone my emotions. There was a silence, then a quick thud of boots.

'He's up there,' said someone. They thought I was up in the gallery. My broadcasting station had diffused its slogans confusingly through four speakers. Legs stopped in front of the grille to my right, a woman's. People were sitting on my box. I heard their talk.

'Funny that voice, wasn't it?'

'Gave me the shivers, though.'

'Funny though, what was it saying?'

'Something about hanging that man McAllen, you know, the haystack killer—'

'The moon maniac—'

'He strangled this girl in this haystack.'

'That's funny.'

'You wouldn't think it was funny if it happened to you.'

'Don't have any haystack where I come from. Never saw a haystack in Manchester—'

'Plenty of sex maniacs, though—'

63

'Men are all the same. He stole her handbag too.'

'They'll do anything.'

'Never saw a haystack in Manchester, though. Just a Corn Exchange.'

Just a corn exchange. I lowered myself to the floor, trying to calculate the time. Then I stamped out of the Museum, slamming all the many doors behind me, hurting no one, preaching to no one, keeping my feet moving fast and my head steady. The Museum clock told me it was time for Tom's first informal rehearsal, probably the only one this week, for the regulars were rehearsing for next week's *Murder at Maggotsfield*. As I paused outside the Acorn, I saw a kind of vision: Sheila. Brighter than a new bus in the sun, she made the grey, black, tan traffic as unimportant as a foraging procession of ants. If I had been in the offices along her route I would have torn up ticker-tape machines and telephones for Broadway confetti. Happiness is usually only something to remember, but that day I recognized it and saluted as it approached. It was like very smooth whisky, as if I were a distillery producing the golden stuff.

'Where have you been?' I asked, without meaning to.

'Cooking for Ben.' There was a pang of anger until I remembered that Ben was her brother. 'You look ruddy.'

'I'm happy, that's all.'

'Everyone's happy. There's more money about. You can get a washing machine for six month's hard labour and easy instalments. Don't boast about being happy.'

'Are you happy?'

She looked at me and widened her wide eyes. 'I'll let you know.' We walked into the theatre arm in arm.

The first number was 'Song for Scientists'. Four of us stood in a stiff row like revue artists, while Tom sat in the stalls, his back curved like a tortoise's and his neck forward, hands coiled ready to spring out into applauding or supplicating gestures. I began my verse as Velma nudged me:

> 'Sir John took the secret from the atom
> Like a winkle from its shell,
> Einstein did a theory of the universe
> And he did it jolly well.
> Pavlov invented saliva
> With a doggie and a bell—'

'Cough, cough, you're drowning the piano,' said Tom. Deliberately I made my face look sad. I felt like singing with my whole voice, the piano needed drowning.

'Let's have more of the words and less of the voice on this one, speak it more. You can't sing it all, speak some of it.'

Remembering the great tradition of singers—Gene Kelly, Marlon Brando, Marlene Dietrich, Fred Astaire, Eartha Kitt and Rex Harrison—I droned a bit, hitting the odd musical note just for variety. That pleased Tom. Velma began her verse:

> 'Fleming couldn't eat his jelly,
> So penicillin grew—'

'Too soft, darling, give it some edge. I won't stop you again.'

It was time for the number I wanted, a duet with Sheila.

'Now you're miles apart,' said Tom. 'It's raining hard outside, and you, Johnny, call up Sheila. I want it slow, but not too grim to start with; keep the grisliness for the last verse.'

Sheila stood down right, leaning. She would have been looking into my eyes if I had been seven feet taller. I brought the imaginary telephone close to my lips, looked upwards and began:

> 'Oh, the Gulf Stream crosses the Atlantic Ocean,
> Warming Britain, France and Portugal and Spain.
> And the trade winds fly across the ocean
> And they bring the soft, warm rain.'

Sheila's voice burst slowly into flame over the mild-tempered piano:

'It's raining on my hotel down in Plymouth,
It's pouring on your flat in Potters Bar,
But much as I would love to come and see you, hold
    you,
I'll stay where I am—you stay where you are
And
Don't go out in the rain, darling,
For the rain is thick in the air.
Don't go out in the rain, darling,
It's falling everywhere—'

'Even slower,' said Tom. 'And Sheila, next to last line of the intro, where did that "hold you" come from? Very pretty.'

'I felt like it.'

'Keep it in for the moment. And both of you, a little less of the Ella Fitzgerald, bit more of the Vera Lynn. It's a nice simple melody, let's keep it that way.'

On dragged the love-song, to reveal that the lovers shared a chronic fear of fall-out. As Sheila sang it was terrifying the way she never looked at me, kept looking up for the rain on the roof. She took it so slowly you wanted to cry out for the next bar. Her voice burned me, I was cooked. The rehearsal stumbled to a close.

Sheila was looking at me across the café table, her mouth awash with fried egg. Roger warmed his hands round a cup of black instant coffee, sugar sprinkled generously in its saucer; Roger seldom ate. Velma hummed quietly like a teleprinter. In the early summer evening outside, the shadow of a five-foot woman was twelve feet long, jerking along behind her. The light around the shadows was yellowing. Roger began to talk:

'What happened to you this morning, actor?'

'I got sick of Devon. James Devon,' I explained to Sheila. 'We were having a drink.'

'Armpit Jimmy,' said Roger.

'He wants this man McAllen to hang.'

'Man, you can't get sick every time Devon opens his dirty mouth. It never closes.'

'In a Garden of Fragrance for the Blind, Devon would spend his nights spreading crap all over the flower-beds,' I said.

'Why Devon?' asked Sheila. 'Why hate him particularly?'

'He sums it up.'

'But he's not a symbol. He may be a Tory, but he's a man of some sort.'

'If that's a man, I'm resigning,' said Roger.

I was angry. 'He wants to hang McAllen. He'd like to do it himself.'

'I don't know McAllen,' said Sheila.

'Do you want them to hang people?'

Sheila gave me a distant, hurt look. I felt a pain. I handed her my petition as a test. She read the carboned words carefully twice, then signed it with a fat-nibbed, mottled pen. I folded it into the grimy envelope I had ready, addressed it to the Home Secretary. I tried to explain Devon.

'You can ignore him,' said Sheila. 'You can switch him off.'

'But people don't switch him off, they listen to him. Look, sometimes a man gets so tangled up in his ideas that he becomes an idea himself. Like Sir Anthony Eden became Suez. Whatever happened to him, anyway? If you like a painter's work enough, you like the painter. Devon's like that. Devon's reached that stage. His message is that people are nice, that the Tory Party is full of nice people because it is the party of people who know their place, honest people who set the prosperity of their country above the rat-race of party politics and ideals. Devon's ideal, his only ideal, is the public personality of Devon. Devon, Man of Justice, recreating murder trials as an awful warning to us all; Devon, the Man of the Country, the common-sense sod who brings a breath of the farmyard into the slum parlour; Devon, the Problem Solver, advising chastity. A highly political institution.'

'He talks contentment like soldiers talk sex,' said Roger. 'Contented stupor for the stupid. Billy Graham, Norman Vincent Peale, Godfrey Winn, Edgar Lustgarten, Ralph Wightman, Charles Curran are one thing. St James Devon is in a class by himself. The ball and chain on the laziest people in the world. Mr Complacency.'

'There's nothing like him,' I said. 'Nothing I've ever met. He manages to appear holy and bloodthirsty at the same time. In an argument he weighs his opponent carefully first. If the man's a lightweight Devon mangles him horribly, puts his foot on the man's chest, and howls for God and Lord Palmerston to flap down from heaven and pick the victim clean. If it's someone who can out-think him, he lets him argue, an ordinary-chap expression on his face and bluffing questions thrown in all the way. When the man leaves, he turns to the company. "Of course he certainly is a strong personality," says Devon. Then the smears start.

'At the end of one of these sessions he looked at me as a Liberal girl walked out, and said in a low voice: "She can't get it off her mind, you know." "What?" "I thought everyone knew," he said. "Perhaps I oughtn't to tell you, but as an old friend of the family . . . She's actually in love with her brother. Awful business." '

'Was she?'

'Of course she was. I knew her well. She fell in love with this brother of hers and he could never understand why she wouldn't see him. She killed herself in the end. She told me about her brother when she was trying to find out what to do. I could never get revolted at all about incest. It always seemed fair enough. I wasn't much help. I'd been reading a novel and told her to start a new life in Australia. She told me her other brother lived in Australia.'

'What did you do?'

'I still thought she should go abroad and I lent her a little money. But she couldn't go. I was half in love with her then, and planned to get her to fall in love with me. That didn't work. Devon never did a damn thing except stir it up for her.'

'I can see him on Personal Problem trying to sort that one out,' said Roger. He blurred and deepened his voice. 'Well, well, I am old-fashioned enough to be a little shocked by this particular problem, but I think I can understand the position. This young lady, Bugged of Belston, must really realize that this sort of thing just won't wash. She must face the fact that a little Christian self-denial would not be out of place. She should certainly talk to her priest, family doctor or milkman. Cold baths, tennis, a job with horses, a rambling club attached to her local Sunday School, dancing, jellies and a little canvassing with the Young Conservatives. And if that doesn't cure her, and pesonally I haven't much faith in the psychological approach, I should say a good sound thrashing, delivered by her priest, family doctor and milkman.'

Someone was licking my hand under the table. It was God, woken by his master's penetrating voice.

'Millions love old Devon,' I said. 'That makes it worse. One day I was drinking in a country pub. An electric thrill, zammee, ran through the public bar when I mentioned I knew Devon. They were all fans. They persuaded me to ring him up so one of them could talk to him. I chose an old man with a fat nose who tried to sell Devon some special preparation for his farm.'

'Millions love old Devon, who do you love?' That was Sheila's peaceful voice.

'Six o'clock. Christ, I'm off to the Unicorn. Come along, Velma,' said Roger. Velma paused. I said nothing, just smiled and nodded.

'Tomorrow night,' said Roger. 'My night off. Hate session at my place. Bring bottles.'

'All right.' They left.

'Well, who do you love?'

'You mean famous people?' Sheila was laughing. I listed them: 'Um, Ella Fitzgerald, Michael Foot, Sarah,

Ellington, Basie, Joe Turner, Jimmy Rushing, Thurber, Miles Davis. My sister, my brother, Ben, sometimes Velma a bit, sometimes even Roger when he makes me laugh. Some dead people. I love you.'

The table-cloth was the colour of freshly-bled blood. The tea was the same colour as the stained wooden walls. The floor under my shoes was hard. I considered my hands. My hands are two well-trained animals and their tricks are multitudinous as the emotions at a carnival. They are in form, but not in hardness, like the hands of a trade unionist who once, when a red coal jumped from the grate at a Labour Party meeting, took the coal between his work-hardened thumb and forefinger and placed it back in the fire. The ceiling was the colour of the tea. I considered my hands. They were too stubby to interest Dürer, too grubby to impress Florence Nightingale, too delinquent to please Lord Goddard. Unless he decided to hack and smooth out a grossly comic carving for a change, Rodin would not have dug them. These hands are divided into hard zones where the skin is near the bone, soft zones where the flesh is deep, and the insensitive zones where nicotine has anaesthetized the little nerves. The nails are almost circular, tough and brittle at the same time. I repeated my early warning.

'I love you,' I said.

'Till when?' she said, looking at her watch.

'I love you.'

'It's not that simple, is it?'

'It ought to be simple, it damn well ought to be simple. Even when it's simple it's complicated enough. There's enough difficulty in working, staying alive, without love being full of difficulties as well.'

As I sat smoking I thought I saw out of the corner of my left eye a white dog padding silently across the floor. It was only the smoke from my cigarette.

'Simple,' she said. 'Simple. I love that word, but I've never seen anything simple.'

'Not even Devon's grand passion for the public?'

70

'No. I don't know him and I bet you don't. He probably gives thousands anonymously to refugees.'

'He doesn't. He gave them twenty pounds publicly the other night on Charity of the Week. Of course I recognize that he's a great man. His cultural influence pervades the intellectual cosmos of our time. He has only to take off his socks and new renaissance sweeps through the arts and sciences. Shall I sing you a song called "Off With Your Trousers and On with the Dance"?'

'Yes, if it'll help get Devon the hell out of this conversation.'

'I wish I'd waited to say I love you.'

'Have you changed your mind?' She looked again at her watch.

'No, but I should have kept it. I should have said other things first. Like, You have a pretty dress. And that's nice perfume. And you look pretty tonight. And here's a big box of chocolates. And here's a bunch of purple flowers, I picked them myself. And let's go for a train ride, how about Brighton? And this is a nice hotel, my room's number 41, what's yours? And my father acts, sometimes I make a thousand a year, what's your blood group? And then I might have got around to it, but I'm too impatient. Bad at courting.'

'And I ought to say, Let me be like a sister—'

'I've got a sister—'

'You talk a lot—'

'No, just when I'm excited. You excite me. So I talk a lot.'

'I'll listen. I like it.'

That made it difficult to talk. 'As I was saying,' I began heartily, then mumbled, 'I love you. I know love usually goes wrong, like The dog comes to the gate. His name is Ro-ver. Shei-la o-pens the gate. Ro-ver eats Shei-la. The dog jumps over the gate. Bad Ro-ver. It's not like that, you know, it's not like that. It's more like being blindfold and trying to keep moving towards your voice.'

71

She touched my hand for a moment. I was telling the truth, discovering the truth as I talked.

'Take me to the theatre,' she said. So we went to watch the boys and girls run through Act One of *Murder at Maggotsfield*, a quick rehearsal before the evening performance of *House Party*. Since both plays were set in country houses, the set was congruous. The curtain rose on the drawing-room of Maggotsfield Manse, pronounced Maunsfield Muggins, home of Lady Charlieworthy, pronounced Chewley, a stately home to which only people who want to murder each other are ever invited.

Lord Clabbertate came in and switched on the chandelier. He walked round the stage, looking at the settee, the radio, the cocktail cabinet, picking up and putting down a cigarette case, rearranging the flowers, picking up a long silver paper-knife and putting it down again, leaving finger-prints everywhere, lighting a cigarette and walking out through the french window. In came Simone the maid. She started to dust the room, picking up the cigarette case and the paper-knife as she did so. The telephone rang convincingly.

SIMONE (*into telephone*): Allo, Allo. Oui, this is Maunsfield Muggins, 'ome of Lady Chewley. Certain there are several people staying 'ere. Eh bien, there is Lady Chewley of course, she is rather—'ow you say?—eccentrique, and come to think of it all of them 'ere are rather a rummy lot. There is that young Jim Blades, ah so 'andsome, ze tennis champion. There is the Reverend Joshua Stonegall 'oo talks so much of religion, but of course 'e is not staying, 'e just comes in when 'e feels like it. (*Simone plumped the cushions absently with her free hand, an old stage habit. Lady Chewley entered and stood in the doorway to listen unobserved.*) Zere is Lord Clabbertate 'oo just went out through the window française, and two jeune filles, Lady June and Lady May, of course they 'ave both been married to Desmond Kale. Yes, 'e is 'ere as well. And Colonel Gumble, quel homme, 'e's been East and knows all about

Chinese poisons. Oui, Miss Marbles, I'm sure it will be all right if you come round in about ten minutes. (*As Simone put down the receiver there was a shot offstage. Simone jumped.*)

LADY CHEWLEY: You should know by now, Simone, that the ferryman always sounds his gun five minutes before the hour, seven minutes before he crosses the bight. To whom were you talking on the telephone?

SIMONE: Nobody, your ladyship. Well, only Miss Marbles.

LADY CHEWLEY: What, that old—

(*Another shot was heard.*)

SHEILA: I love you a bit, Johnny.

We went to Brady's. Brady's head is thin and long, Brady's hands are narrow, Brady's mouth is thin and long, Brady's eyes are narrow. Brady believes in little except the drink. His pub was rebuilt in 1952 when the Festival of Britain was doing terrible things in the mind of Brady, and it will still be contemporary when Covent Garden plays Martian operas. The Martians will probably have a better time of it than the humans at Brady's, what with triangular doors, sloping floors and a psychiatrist's couch which Brady bought from a psychiatrist. You feel drunk before your first drink. We stood with our backs to the one reminder of Queen Victoria, the heart of oak, history-dark bar, and looked at each other like two lost children.

'What shall we do, Sheila? This looks like a good night.'

'We'll drink and talk and get to know each other.'

'Simple, you see, it is simple.'

'Yes, it is,' she said.

We began to talk. I learned more about her when we sang together, but Brady discouraged anything so lively. He had no licence for singing, and black-printed notices reminded us. She told me about some men.

'He thought I was quiet as first, and so I was, but then I got noisy. He had to think, he didn't want to talk. Then he had to stay in the same place to think, so we couldn't

73

go out together. Then he wanted to stay in bed all the time he wasn't working. I don't like eating meals in bed. So that finished that.'

I told her about some women. I discovered I could tell her nothing but the truth. If you could square a circle, that might be the shape of her face, not round, not square, certainly not oval, the black eyebrows almost colliding on her white forehead. We talked jazz. She shakes when she laughs aloud; she often laughs aloud. We talked politics and she made a deep-toned political speech ending:

'. . . I assure you, my friends, I promise you, that if you return me to Parliament even the field mice will have bicycles.'

We talked of Harold Macmillan. Her breasts were impossible to ignore, only three-quarters covered by her furry brown smock. I tried to keep my eyes on her eyes. We talked of Harold Macmillan and his bomb. The conversation slowed and bumped along as we talked of love, smoking more than usual. She asked me about my getting sick with all this killing, Ben had told her something. It seemed a small thing. I told it with gags to make it even smaller.

Sheila's flat was in the same block as Joan's. It had one enormous window facing the street, and when we pushed through the door side by side all I could see were the crimson and black curtains, painted with fabulous birds, beasts and stars in white and light blue. They were large and clumsy, those creatures, they cavorted among the stars. A street lamp lit them from behind, lending them a kind of glow. When Sheila switched on the mild lights at each side of the room, the glow left the curtains and seemed to settle on her. Apart from a blue thick rug in front of the electric fire, the floor was covered in black lino. She had chalked elephants on the lino, the chalk came off on my shoes. There were small paper books everywhere, a modern div. in bed, a wooden chair, a string chair, a modern divan bed, a crate of dark, sticky ale and a modern divan bed.

I was telling myself, drink up this nice beer and go home, there are weeks of rehearsal and performance ahead of you, and she was probably telling herself, drink up this nice beer and send him home. Home, whatever that meant. Home is a state of mind. Charity begins there. Charity ends there. Home is where Mother Machree lived, there is no place like it. Home is where, if foreigners don't like it here, they should go. No chariot swings low for to carry me there, no chariot swings this low. Home is where I hang my brother. Home is a cold bed in a room on your own with cold and cold running water. There are no more at home like me. Home are the old folks, home from the sea, and the terrible hunter home from the hill. Home is where you start from, and when you get ragged and hungry and nasty and sick, a home is where they put you.

I worked it out like that until I ran out of homes to tear down and thought of my home, that square room with fictional flowers on the paper, when we drifted together and started to dance to the music in our heads. The music was slow, we sank closer together and found ourselves standing still in the middle of the room, holding each other desperately.

WEDNESDAY

'WILL YOU WAIT for me here?'

I had the feeling that one of her songs like high waves rolling might roar up in Sheila and sweep her to any place in the world. She was such a clear figure in my imagination now that I didn't have to shut my eyes to see her in any scenery, involved in any action.

'I think I'll stay.'

She smiled. I had no chalk to draw a circle round her in a magic way. I stepped into the street and my head cleared, I recognized myself in a new part. A missionary, come to a new land by accident, by happy shipwreck. Missionaries hand out beads. The natives closed their eyes in careful prayer while the missionary feverishly heaved the Union Jack to the top of the coconut tree. I wanted to convert Sheila entirely to me, but flags and beads were not enough. I still had a lot of money.

Within fifteen minutes I had bought a car, for courting within the city limits is drab. It was a shanty on wheels and I knew where to buy it. Simon Markham had been trying to sell it for £45 for three months; he took £40 from me. In a toyshop I bought a Scottish standard for the bonnet made of probably handwoven paper. The red lion was very rampant, and it tickled my nostalgia for the Scotland I had never seen. There was a tin seal in the shop as well, as smooth as Sheila, with a coloured ball on its nose. The seal was the bluish colour of a gun, you could

77

push it and the gears gave it speed, the ball revolved, the flippers flipped. I bought the seal. There was the James Devon Murder Trial Game, based loosely on the Underarm Odour King's TV series on famous trials. The game involves cards with alibis and clues, as well as little hunted plastic figures moulded in running postures which you push around a board. The game ends when the loser is hanged. Instead I bought Nationalization, a kind of Monopoly for socialists. Next door in the sweetshop I bought some heart mixture and tried one. It tasted doughy, fizzy and sweet at the same time. Each small heart bore a message—'I LOVE YOU' or 'NAUGHTY BOY' or 'ASK ME AGAIN' or 'CHEEKY'. I bought equipment at the chemist's. In the off-licence I found some wine that I knew was strong for the price, two bottles. An L.P. by a demolition squad led by Thelonious Monk; I wrote 'YES LOVE' in big letters on the back of the sleeve. I bought her a petticoat in the colour of Welfare Orange Juice, and books of poems by Anthony Thwaite and Christopher Logue. In my excitement I could feel indigestion rising in subterranean bubbles. I get indigestion like Japan gets earthquakes, especially at auditions. Then Refinement hides its head, Good Manners leaves the room and Discrimination starts discriminating against me as the audition draws to an explosive, farting close. After sniffing around among twenty bottles of scent, I chose one in the depths of whose aroma seemed to lurk warm-coloured, graceful creatures, blue and orange deer on an island of spice trees. Another sniff, and a family of unicorns walked up one nostril and down the other, multicoloured rain fell in my head. I paid, then looked at the label. It was called Diggez-Moi, For Teenagers. I bought two pounds of apples, a honeycomb, a pewter bracelet on which squat figures, probably Sinhalese, tooted and strummed musical instruments shaped like odd fruits.

Sheila laughed as I laid my gifts at her feet in traditional style. She swirled in the petticoat, sucked two sweets, clipped on the bracelet and crunched an apple. She put on a great deal of scent. She had to go to London to see an

78

agent about her singing, but we had an hour before the train. We drove up to the thin grass covering the highest point of the cliffs. Belston looked flat, the yellow chunk of Blooter's dominating the dark-grey spike of the cathedral spire. On a near-by bench a long huddle of brown macintosh stirred and two eyes stared at us. Without haste the shape reformed into the figure of a standing, bearded man, his face tanned to the colour of brown boot-polish, his left hand holding a hairy string from which depended a half-empty bottle of some clear liquid. He approached with big, meaningful strides.

'Can you let me have some fags?' he asked, without a shade of apology in his voice; the answer seemed to hang on whether we had any cigarettes. I've been out of work too, so my only pause was to look at him.

'You can call it begging if you like, but I can tell you things.'

Everyone wants to tell me things, but Sheila sank her chin against her neck as if she wanted to be told.

'What's your name?' she asked.

'Now that's one thing you shouldn't ask, you know you shouldn't ask that. They call me Perfect.' He nodded as if approving the unlikely name. 'Not because of my ways, you know. But when I worked at the Zoo they always asked me what sort of day I had and I always said "Perfect." It's a word I like. I once won three quid on a dog called Perfect Lady.'

'Why did you leave the Zoo?'

'Ah.' He sat down and took a cigarette. 'You see, I was on nights. All very well, you might say. Walking round between the cages and cases, seeing the snakes didn't eat each other, listening for noises. Now I'm not a drinking man, you know, not much of a drinking man, but it got on my nerves. All those noises. So on pay night I used to take a bottle in with me. That was better. I walked round and made noises back at the animals. Sing to some of them I did. Well, one night I was singing to this chimp and she grabbed the bottle. Swigged it down. That got me thinking, perhaps the animals could use a drop now and then. They got nerves, you know. I found that a lot of them wouldn't touch it. I had to stick to mammals, of course. Llamas get hiccups, you know, and hogs just roll about. The best ones to drink with were the chimps. I gave it them in plastic beakers. But they found me one morning flat in the chimp cage. Sally, she was the big chimp, was staggering about in my hat. I had to leave. Under a cloud, you know.'

'What did you do then?' I asked, for the question was expected.

'I sat down to think. I worked out that I should be a beachcomber, but I was inland. I worked it out. Do you know how much you waste in one week?'

We both said no.

'I worked it out. In one week I got rid of the Cellophane, silver paper, cardboard and butts from five packets of twenty, when I was earning, you understand. Two meat bones, three or four tins, an ounce of fat, match-sticks, two or three bits of stale bread, five empty bottles, four newspapers, not to mention dirt and sweat. If a poor man turns out that much in a week, how much does an ordinary working man leave behind, or a luxury man? I tell you, five times as much. I live simple. I can live on the dustbins of one classy street.'

He pointed to a cardboard box full of grubby gleanings. I realized that he looked something like me. I didn't like him, but he seemed to act something like me as well. Like him, I spent most of my time pleasing myself, letting my mind run wild, living on shaky wits, calling myself perfect. I had to get drunk now and then, though I never carried surgical spirit in a bottle on the end of a string. I promised myself to aim at a steady income, to become a successful singer by the end of the year. Perfect put on the pressure for a contribution. He shuffled towards the cliff with despair working on his face, a silent threat of suicide on his mouth. We saved him with a ten-shilling note, though the world was over-populated and we knew he would have

watched us jump hand in hand over the edge, interested
only in what he could salvage at the bottom. Slowly he
walked away, husbanding his strength, which was probably
still considerable. Sheila and I drove quietly to the station.
We sat looking at steam through the dirty glass of the
buffet.

'Did you notice his nose?' said Sheila.

'What about it?'

'He had a good nose.'

'I don't usually notice noses. Did you see his eyeballs?
Scribbled all over with red lines.'

'I don't suppose he sleeps much.'

'I sleep a lot.'

The conversation stopped. We were finding it hard
to talk about ourselves, we were so ignorant of each
other.

'Who's the agent?' I asked.

'Fernley,' she said. 'If that doesn't work I'll call on
Gerry Dunne. I heard he wants to promote some British
jazz.'

'He's a gambler.'

'Don't you like gambling? I used to bet every day, on
some horse, but the fun wore off.'

'I don't mind gambling but I usually spend money on
solid things. Betting's like buying an abstraction.'

'Abstraction?'

'Money's a kind of abstraction; as soon as I get it I like
to convert it into something real.'

She laughed at me and I liked it.

'When do you come back?' I said.

'Early tomorrow morning. I'll come straight to you,
Johnny.'

'Where are you staying?'

'With two girls called Louise in Earls Court. Hogarth
Road.'

'That doesn't sound safe.'

'Where are you sleeping?'

'At home. Look, I love you, I'm safe.'

'So am I, so am I safe. I don't make promises like this, but you can trust me this once, love.'

'I'm sorry, I didn't mean to talk like a keeper. Don't make any promises.'

She was leaning from the compartment window, kissing my face.

'Good luck,' I shouted as the train trundled away from me. The station was coated in dirt. I posted the petition to the Home Secretary. I had followed the McAllen trial very closely. I hate the law, those trial rooms with their polished wooden boxes. A man in a box with a book in his hand, mumbling, and another man in a box with his eight fingers along the yellow rail, and the long wooden box with twelve people who long for sausages and warm beverages round the home fire and the fat cat. They sit in two rows watching the man in the dock, thinking thoughts about him:

The man in the dock has a name like the name of the man who lived next door and had to move, he had to move they say. The man had a bad shave today. The man has poorly developed arm muscles, but a strong neck, what there is of his neck, what you can see of his neck, his neck, it looks strong. The man wears expensive clothes, too expensive. He is too ordinary for words. He has no words. The man does not chew gum, we would hate him more if he chewed gum, he would not be allowed, surely they wouldn't let him chew gum in court. The man stands behind his hands, which clench on the yellow rail. Justice makes him sweat, and the wet mist from his palms of his hands remains on the yellow rail after the man has gone down the stone stairs to eat what he can for lunch. I expect the man would like to be in a boat, not as a pirate or fugitive, but just afloat under some sun. The man has poison under his skin, you can tell, it is swelling into small spots on his face. He lost his temper when they asked about the passport, you could see him change; his humidity changed, he became very humid.

The man's cousel has a wig like the inside of the mattress on the rubbish dump, the Council should have it burnt. He has worn the wig for many years and could afford a new one, but his curving red cheeks would look almost youthful under a clean wig. His voice is embarrassingly alto, cracking on the top notes, his books are in heavy towers at his hand, he believes that wit is an essential ingredient of the good defence. The court officials and reporters rock with pleasure at his sallies, the unsophisticated relatives in the gallery sit with rattled smiles.

COUNSEL: If your Lordship pleases, I should be very pleased.
(*Laughter.*)
JUDGE: You would please your client, I suspect, if you pleased me more.
(*Laughter. Faint cheers.*)
COUNSEL: If you please.
(*General hysteria.*)
JUDGE: I don't bring pleas, please.
(*Insurrection.*)

Thus barristers and judges aim to be proper little Henry Cecils. They nearly all succeed. The shorthand-writer's right hand glides and stabs over the paper, then her left hand flicks over another page.

On the way back to my room I saw the broad shoulders of Ford swinging along the pavement. I parked the car and caught up with him. We stood by a bus stop, apparently locked in metaphysical harmony like Wordsworth and Coleridge, while we watched the girls go by. I supposed Ford was still carrying the knife. His aesthetics rumbled and became audible.

'There's a pretty sight. Now that really is cute. Watch it twitch like that. There's a girl who really moves it. Wonder how she rates head-on. Guess I'll never know. But dig that twitch. That really is my thought for today.'

A wild-looking dog, all hair and tail, galloped up to us

and began to lick the thin layer of salt off Ford's hand.
Ford patted its nose without much trust. A woman who
had formed a queue behind us, her arms cuddling a pot-
bellied pekinese, muttered aloud:

'That dog looks like a fighter to me. He should be on a
lead.'

Ford looked concerned.

'No, lady,' he said. 'This ain't a fightin' dog.'

'He looks like it.'

'This ain't a fightin' dog, he's a lovin' dog.' She looked
away. 'Well, use your eyes, lady. He ain't no fightin' dog.
Your pussy-cat is safe enough.' A small man emerged
from behind the woman.

'My wife's quite right. You should have that dog on a
lead.'

'Your wife?'

'My wife's quite right.'

'Look,' said Ford with an edge of exasperation in his
slow voice, 'now look now. I was just standing watching
the women—no, not your wife, just the women—and this
dog comes up. He ain't my dog, never seen him. I don't
carry aniseed balls to attract dogs, you know.' He looked
accusingly at the man. 'You got aniseed balls, mister?'

The man took a pace forward as his wife stepped aside,
and he touched one of Ford's lapels. Ford raised a heavy,
scarred eyebrow at the wife.

'Call him off, will you?'

The man glared. 'You Yanks come over here and you
take everything.'

Ford was looking at the sky for guidance. I knew he
wouldn't get any so I said: 'I wouldn't touch my brother.'

Ford looked down at the man sadly. 'I'm not in the
mood today, but I'll tell you three things, Archibald, then
you better catch a bus quick. One, that ain't my dog. Two,
I'm not a Yank. Three, get out of my life.'

The dog slunk off as a bus drew up. Ford turned to me.

'That little chick who twitched,' he said. 'Well, if I was
a dame and I had it like that and I knew how much it

was needed around, why, I'd go round handing it out to the men. It's only nice.'

Ford was back in his dream. There had been weeks in which I had never thought of Ford, but I remembered him. Now I knew him again, a sleek-suited tearaway with a skin thicker than a leather jacket, a man who carried a knife and talked like a man who carries a knife. I cast him for Cain, myself for Abel. I never saw Ford in the States and hardly ever saw my father. Father used to send money to me now and again and visit twice a year.

Ford and I went for a Coke. The café was streamlined, as if built to travel fast. We sat at a blue-topped table among about twenty blue-topped tables, mostly empty. I asked Ford about Father.

'Never hear from him. When I was in Chi, when I was a kid, he used to write now and then on those coloured postcards. Pictures of Yellowstone Park.'

'Did he visit you often?'

'Kidding? Not once. Not once in the States, except my first week.'

'Well, I assumed he came to visit you.'

'Good. I'm glad you assumed. I assumed he was kept busy. Don't get me wrong. I never much wanted him to come. I wasn't in the house much, anyway, down in the hole with the gang. Cellar under an old woodhouse. We had a museum there, cute. Knives. An old bed too. You know? You'd go to the hardware store, get a kitchen knife with a good strong blade, one that hardly bent, a meat knife, one that balanced well in your hand. Spend a few hours on the stone with it, then it went into stock, sharp. Sharp. I was traveller for the museum. Used to hitch out of town to a store with cheap switch-blades, second-hand. Hitched with a cop once. I had five blades in my pocket. We used to buy the switches with the money we got selling meat knives to the kids. Cop thought I was running away. I told him no. He sat there like concrete setting, harder and harder. I didn't know what to do, I could see everything he was thinking. I told him I was going home, but he stopped the car. Pulled off my coat, took out the switches and threw them in the lake. Then he knocked me about and left me by the road. Knew I couldn't squeal. He had a kind face. How the hell did he know? I beat him, anyway. I stripped and dived and got four of the switches back.'

'Did you use the knives?'

'Kidding? We were in business. We sold them, charged little kids to look at them. Lots of sales but we were very quiet. Hardly ever used them. We stayed in our own part of town. We were making money.'

'Where's you car, Ford?'

He looked angry. 'Had to sell it,' he said. 'Pay off some money. Gotta pay off a little more, too. You got any money, Johnny? I need another hundred.'

'Dollars?'

'Pounds.'

'Sorry, I can't make it. I had about £85 left of my original £200. I wouldn't be paid until Friday week.'

'You sure?'

'I'm sorry. Is that why you came into town today?'

'Yeah, well, O.K.'

'Ford, you'll be bloody careful in this racket, won't you?'

He snorted. He snorted like some kind of hog.

'Right. You know about me. I smuggle whisky, cigarettes. Does that bother you?'

'I'm not bothered about whether you're legal. But that knife. People get killed.'

'Man, you make me worry, I have to get an apron and mother you? Look at this, what makes you think about killing? I use my brain, man. I'll tell you. You're up against a big system, Johnny, it's so big.'

He was lapsing into inarticulate movie philosophy. I thought it was my chance to get a word in edgeways.

'I'm not fighting any system, Ford.'

He just laughed.

'Not with a knife, anyway.'

86

'No, Johnny, you got enough trouble anyway. You keep out. Keep clean. You keep outside, do some singing, you'll be happy as a daisy-chain. Well, all right then. So the system is big, bigger than me and bigger than you, and it's a big sweat to stop the system messing us. So the system is bigger but it can't move so fast. I keep way out of reach. Goliath had the weight but David had the gimmick. So you make money by singing like a hippo on heat? Does that make you St Francis?'

Ford's hand was bouncing on the table, powered by the small but well-developed muscles of his fingers. For the third time an aristocratic waitress passed us. Next time she didn't pass. Ford, who wanted his Coke, nodded, slid a chair across the plastic tiles in front of the girl, and snapped: 'Two Cokes.'

The girl looked at him, turned about and retreated through a door without a handle. Out came the manager. He was the same size and build as Ford. Ford's hair looked dead black with a touch of blue under the fluorescent lights; the manager was pale as straw with eyes that seemed to have unlimited range. Given a fight, I wouldn't be sure which to bet on, unarmed combat of course. The manager blinked at Ford, who didn't blink or even look up after he had photographed his opponent out of the corner of his eye, his left hand playing with the cruet like a chess-player gloating self-restrainedly after winning the first game, rearranging the pieces to see if he could possibly have been beaten.

'Have you a complaint to make?'

'I'll have two Cokes.'

'I'm afraid I must ask you not to bother the waitresses.'

'Two Cokes.' The salt-cellar in Ford's hand jumped over the pepper-pot and crashed squarely on the table.

'I'm afraid I must ask you—'

'You cater for parties here? Manage Cokes for twenty or so?'

'I thought you wanted two.'

'Was thinking, I was thinking, maybe we'll bring some friends next time. Or maybe we'll just stay here late for kicks, see what comes. We're certainly staying until we get two Cokes.'

'Two Cokes,' called the manager. 'And if I see either of you in here again making trouble, I'll call the police.'

Ford laughed as the manager walked away, he laughed again as a different waitress brought the syrupy drinks. We drained the tough little bottles. The cashier muttered as I paid. Ford laughed once more, but as I said goodbye to him, brown worry seemed to settle on him.

I ate and drank quietly and politely with myself in Brady's until it was time to take a bottle to Roger's. I was second down to his basement. It was a terrible room. The walls were a piercing yellow. There were no curtains, the centre of the room was bare except for a small carpet, a worn green like a lawn in summer. Round the walls in an oblong line were ranged all the pieces of furniture and all Roger's own possessions, a fence of objects round an empty square space. Roger was sitting on the bed, thinking and drinking. Velma, who always sat on the floor, was sitting on the floor.

'Are we going to dance?' I asked.

'Certainly not,' said Roger. 'Nobody dances here. Dancing is disgusting; it excites the basest instincts, of which you have plenty. You would do better to pray.'

'Why clear the floor then?' I asked blankly. Arranged round the room in this order were these objects: an armchair, a bed, a bicycle, bottles of all kinds, full and empty, an Angela Brazil omnibus, a loaf of bread, a packet of butter, three chairs, one chamber-pot, a chest of drawers, four cups, a bag of eggs, an electric fire, seven forks in a box, Galsworthy's *Forsyte Saga*, eight glasses, back numbers of the *Illustrated London News*, an ink bottle, five knives, letters opened and unopened, Longfellow's *Hiawatha*, half a bottle of milk, a pound note and three pennies, old newspapers, the *Poems of Henry Newbolt*, two oranges, eleven plates, an economy-size packet of New Soggo, five spoons, a stove, a packet of sugar, Dean Swift's works, a table, two towels, a wardrobe, a wash-basin and a waste-paper basket.

'All this belongs to me,' said Roger, moving his arm in a circular gesture which seemed to include Velma, 'and little luck it brings me. I used to lie awake gloating over it, all my wealth, all my pretty possessions. You know, I used to polish things with polish, dust and rearrange ornaments. When I had money I used to go out and buy another object to own. But it weighed me down, I got worried about it, I wanted to dominate the room myself, to show the objects who was boss. So I got rid of most of my things, in dustbins or jumble sales. The things I had to keep I rearranged. To show how much I despised them as personalities, I put them in strictly alphabetical order round the room.'

'That must be awkward. Meals must take hours.'

'You bloody prose actor, of course it's awkward. Any idealist has to make sacrifices. Anyone can live graciously, but what does it prove? Here's a present for you. Had it taken last week.'

He threw me a photograph of himself. Somehow Roger had obtained a life-size reproduction of Annigoni's portrait of the Queen, had cut out the face and stuck his grinning face through the hole. It was as sublime as anything of its kind. Roger's face has the quality of a gargoyle in a cathedral lavatory, and his behaviour matches it. Nobody went to Roger's for the sake of peace and quiet; they came to give performances, and often enough the evening would end in a fight. I like performing and I like to be where the action is, where things are moving. One by one and two by two they arrived. A schizophrenic with his guitar, five mixed undergraduates I didn't know, Simon Markham looking sad, a girl called Fleur who looked like a kind of beat Queen Mother, and a haggard, benzedrined reporter whom everyone called Man. We drank for a while.

First to perform was Fleur, who gave a short, dynamic lecture-demonstration called 'How to Kick a Dog'. In his unalphabetical position between the spoons and the stove,

Roger's God dozed indifferently. Then came a television sketch by the students. Their leader was dressed as the Bishop of Belston. He faced to viewers in full regalia, smiling confidently.

'Good evening, flock. I'd like to tell you a story, an unusual story I grant you, but every word of it is gospel. It happened to a young man on his wedding-day—and I was that young man.'

They arranged themselves in a wedding-reception group, all wearing dog-collars, all sipping gloomily from glasses.

BISHOP: What was wrong? It was the wine.

GUEST A: This wine's got no body in it. It's more like water.

GUESTS (*mumbling*): More like water. This wine's no good.

(*A sudden pause. One voice emerged from the mumble.*)

GUEST B: Jesus Christ, what shall we do about this bloody wine?

(*A man in biblical costume with a thin face and scraggy beard pushed through.*)

MAN IN BEARD: I think I know.

(*He made passes with his hands.*)

GUEST A (*sipping*): Ah, that's better.

GUEST B (*sipping*): That's stronger.

MAN IN BEARD: That's Shamlam. Shamlam, the new miracle drink.

BISHOP: It's divine. Shamlam, you say it's called?

MAN IN BEARD: Yes, Shamlam. Remember the name— you'll never forget the hangover.

GUEST A: It's better.

GUEST B: It's stronger.

MAN IN BEARD: It's consecrated.

(*The Bishop stepped forward.*)

BISHOP: We never discovered who that young man was, but he certainly made my wedding-day memorable. Since then we've switched to Shamlam at Belston and doubled the number of communicants. (*He held up a glass for a toast*.) Blessed are the pure in Hartlepools. Shamlam. The drink with a soul. Shamlam.

Roger seemed inspired by this. He borrowed a dog collar and began to bumble:

'Ah bless you, bless you, bless you. Let's have a little less sneezing from now on. Hallo once again, kneelers, and welcome once more to the Secular Church of Roger Blester. This week we've got something special for you and I hope you're all going to demonstrate your faith, and maybe we'll be able to raise your own Labour Party from the dead. You may be wondering what a lowly mummer is doing here, his name's Johnny Crane. He's an acolyte. All right, all right, he's having treatment for it. If the collection plate comes round, let's be generous, folks. At the Royal Academy dinner here last week we laid on a strip-tease action painter and all the collection brought in was the head of Annigoni on a charger. And remember—Man is an animal (cheers), a spiritual animal (boos), who has become hopelessly corrupted (cheers).'

My mind was circling round Sheila. The drink in the room was evaporating quickly. The reporter read from a list of adjectives used by different newspapers to describe members of the Royal Family. He suggested they might all be replaced by one indisputable adjective—well-to-do. A theological student gave a sermon based on Roger's bicycle. His address concluded:

'Look fairly and see clearly. Of the two wheels of this machine, which possesses the unmarred symbolism which denotes the Hub of Man, the Spokes of pre-History, the Rim of Medievalism, the Tyres of Civilization? It is the first wheel, the former wheel, the wheel which both leads and commands; in its simple grandeur it may be called the true image of Man's Estate. This is the famous wheel of fire, the prayer-wheel of the Tibetans, the wheel of St Catherine, the wheel of fate. In the rear wheel we see a meaner revelation—Man enchained with chains of grit and oil, driven not by love, not by ambition, but by the most ignoble and ludicrous, sparsely-haired and sweating, malodorous and malformed parts of the human body; I mean the feet.'

Fleur began her dance without music. We all sat, envying her invisible partner. Roger was lecturing again on the constructive use of hatred as he lounged on his bed. Leaning against his knees was Velma, lost in some warm little world. Our bedroom scene on Sunday night had been nothing more than an absent-minded welcome back to Belston.

'Any news of Elspeth?' I asked. Roger seemed annoyed.

'Nobody knows. She just got the hell out of Belston.'

'How do you know nobody knows?'

'She was my girl, wasn't she?'

'I'm sorry,' I said. 'I didn't know. I'm going.'

'You want to know something else about Elspeth?'

I just looked at him. I didn't say anything.

'I don't want to know anything else. I'm going.'

Velma blew me a Platonic kiss.

'He's afraid of information,' said Roger. 'Scared of facts. Elspeth is pregnant. My fault.'

'Good night, little sister,' I said to Velma. It was simple, after all, for me if not for Elspeth.

I slept most of the way in the train. Riding through the suburbs of London, that commercial hell, was like having a series of second-class visions. First, through the window of a one-storey, economically constructed office building about ten yards from the track, I saw a thirty-year-old woman sitting upright with her hands covering her eyes; in front of her, on one of forty benches, was one of forty machines, some electronic version of the adding machine. Designed to calculate the cost, the profit, the loss, the value, the dearth—there is no machine can sing. I knew why her hands were tight as bandages over her eyes, or rather, I knew the churning chaos behind those covering hands.

Second, I saw the lights of flats, stacked in vertical piles, and the horizontal stretch of square lights as another train

92

passed us at an angle. There were other lights—cars, small packed houses, cinemas—while below and to the left of my elbow ran another set of rails. I could watch the dullness of their dust-lined, mud-painted flanks, the lengthy gleam of their upper surfaces. They led somewhere. I saw a dim line of black trees, clouds fat with rain. We passed an engine shed, or it might have been a chapel, a clock more brightly lit than the rusty moon, and a garage with its petrol pumps shining out, their heads fierce in the night as the heads of the mad. The train edged up to the platform. I arranged myself on a bench opposite the platform for Belston, and began to wait and sleep and wait for Sheila.

THURSDAY

I WAS FALLING OFF the station bench when Sheila woke me with a cardboard cup of coffee. I strutted up and down to shake the numb parts of my body into life.

'You see, I love you. I didn't know where your doormat was, so I slept on the next best thing.'

'I'm touched.'

'I can't help it. You're compulsive.'

'Good.'

'How were the agents?'

'Fernley wants me to keep in touch. Dunne seemed interested.'

'How interested?'

'Interested.'

'You're a chatterbox this morning. What's the matter?'

'I'm tense.'

'Why?'

'I can see you're tense.'

'I'm sorry. How are Louise and Louise?'

'Interested in Australians. Boomerangs all over the floor.'

I helped her on to the train, then leaned out of our compartment window to keep intruders away. One minute before the train pulled out a neat white man carrying blue flowers approached our door. Using a proved technique, I donned a maniac grin and beckoned to him. He smiled back politely and excused himself as he opened the door

95

and levered himself past me into a corner seat. I smoked a lot of cigarettes. I had been forced to buy tipped ones from the machine and I knew the tobacco was inferior, but I smoked them enthusiastically. Sheila leaned heavily on my shoulder.

'How much do you pay for your room?' she asked.

'Three ten.'

'I pay five for my flat. Let's economize.'

If pearls were seeds, she is the kind of flower that would grow.

'It's logical.'

'Logic is the way crabs think.'

'It's better than logical, it is the only beautiful piece of economics I ever heard. I love you.'

The phrase 'I love you' was becoming frequent as a full stop in my conversation with Sheila. At Belston she stretched her arms and walked towards our flat. I went to collect all my property in the leather bag.

Approaching Mrs Roger's house I stared out of habit at its expressionless brick face. It was expressionless no longer. Curtains were being drawn up and down the house as if night were falling like a bomb. From the pigeon-hole rooms came indignant shouts, some of them brittle with fright. A high window, my window, broke, flowered into javelins and petals of glass which bounced as they slivered again on the pavement. Powdered glass keeps your hair young. The round man from the basement, favourite of Mrs Rogers, padded into the street. His striped shirt was rolled to his elbows, his wrists fat as a baby's. He said without prologue:

'That man's mad. That young man is mad. Get him out.'

'Who's mad?' I asked. Maybe he meant me.

'The man in your room.'

'Doesn't anyone stop madmen getting in my room? Where's Mrs Rogers? Where is the fire brigade?'

'Mrs Rogers is out. That man's breaking your room up. He broke your bed. You oughtn't to let him use your room.'

'I didn't tell anyone they could break my bed.'

'Mr Crane, I'm a family man and I've got responsibilities. There's my little girl. I don't know about you, but I've got a respect for property and law. I've got a good job to keep, I'm not a millionaire, oh no, or an actor either, but it's a steady job, a good job with an old company, and my firm's moving to new premises soon where I'll have a desk by the window.'

I was interested but puzzled. Was this a speech he kept for a special occasion, for any special occasion?

'And that's not all, Mr Crane, that's not the end of it. He broke your window.'

'I saw that. I almost broke it myself last year. You know, there was a bad flaw in the glass, it was too thick just by the frame. When you looked through it, it made people look distorted.'

The man himself began to look distorted, but the bath-water air of love and a summer morning had steamed my head into a happy doze. He continued:

'I went up to reason with him. He wouldn't let me reason. He says he'll tear up your carpet and crucify you with the tacks. That's the way he talked. I wouldn't be surprised if he takes the door with him when he goes. He broke your bed, and your clock.' We had moved into the hall. 'I wouldn't have let him in, he didn't look the sort, only he rang the bell for quarter of an hour and said he was your brother. I was wearing my pyjamas, I couldn't do much. I said he could wait in your room.'

'Maybe he got impatient.'

When I reached the top of the second flight I looked up and saw the door of my room leap open, almost tearing itself away from its hinges. Ford stamped out, his shoulders filling the stairway, mouth an open black oval, eyes crimson, voice roaring and the knife in his right hand.

'Come on up then, Johnny, come on up, Johnny.'

It was me or the cops, so I went up. Ford braced himself against the wall to let me into the room. The bedclothes had been torn off, but the bed still worked. As I walked round the room totting up the damage, Ford, like a goat on a tether, followed behind me, making low noises which could have meant anything. The clock, which I never wound, was entirely broken. The window had nearly all fallen outwards. Half the carpet was up. It had taken three shoes hurled across the room to break the rust-spotted mirror. Drawers had been emptied on the floor, but there was nothing in them but dirty handkerchiefs left by the last lodger and some defunct copies of the *Belston Gazette*. I sat on a clear patch of floor and opened my hands for an explanation.

'You did it all right,' I said. 'You really did it.'

'Money. Money. Now, Johnny, I'm flat. I sold the car. Be good now. I'll have money coming in later.'

'Wrong shop.'

'Hell with that. Man, you'll get some for me? I need eighty quid now. I sold some clothes. I'm sorry, sorry about your room. Look, this is straight. I'm in trouble with some boys who carry knives. Two of them was coming for me, so I got up here. They wanted to come up quiet and take me. Only way I could get help was to kick up hell, it might keep them off or it might get someone in to break it up, even a cop. I thought I'd thrown them off, but they must have found my cab driver. They really want to take me, Johnny. I'm two days late with my payment. I just need eighty now. Then I'm safe. But I need it now. I've quit the base. If I pay this there'll be no more trouble.'

I looked out of the window and there were two pairs of bull shoulders crossing the street. I fancied my new role.

'Stay here,' I said. 'I'll buy your knife for eighty pounds.'

He flicked in the blade and gave it to me. I slipped it in my pocket. The bull shoulders were coming up the stairs and I met them on the first floor. One of them looked as if he had been carsick. The other one wore a big smile. They came very close to me but said nothing. The one with the big smile kept nodding his large head.

'What do you want?'

'Want to see Ford.'

'He's not around.'

'He's upstairs.'

'I'm his brother. Anything I can do?'

'He owes us money.'

'Eighty?'

'Eighty.'

I counted out eighty, almost all I had. It took a very long time. Then I held the green bundle behind my back like an arch nursery-school teacher.

'I'll give it to you somewhere else. At the museum. You can take me there.' I said that loudly so Ford could hear. The museum was the first place I thought of, but they didn't seem to know where it was. 'Or the cliffs,' I said. 'Somewhere quiet. I think the cops are on their way here.'

The three of us climbed in my car and we drove up to the cliffs. The car just made it. As we drove one of them showed me his knife. It was better than mine, a fine piece of craftsmanship, though I didn't say so. I had become Marlon Brando in *On the Waterfront*, they could do what they liked. Without getting out of the car, I paid them the money, then gave them a lift back to their base. At a garage in town I sold my car for thirty-five pounds, enough to carry me through.

Back in my room I found Mrs Rogers. She was weeping carefully into her handkerchief. I felt angry with Ford, I saw him as Cain again, that scar on his eyebrow the little trademark of violence. As Abel, I phoned a glazier for a new window. As Abel, I retacked the carpet and bought a new £4 mirror.

'I'll leave straight away, Mrs Rogers. I'm very sorry.'

'You've paid your rent. It's such a nice room. I never had any trouble.' She stopped crying when I gave her ten pounds for the rest of the damage, then she said it was too much and started crying again. I argued. As I put the debris of my clock in the waste-paper basket I saw a note: 'Dear Johnny, I left town. I'll try to get a job band singing. I got friends in London. I phoned Joan and told her where

I'll be. Sorry. Thanks. I'll see you right. Your brother, Ford. Good luck.' It didn't read like Cain. But I had seen Ford's temper, bulging, ready to burst over the first man to poke it around. When we trudged backwards and forwards over Korea I saw men like Abel on those hills, their uniforms and flesh on fire. I felt the weight of McAllen hanging round my neck.

Holding that wrinkled leather bag, I walked down Gladstone Street. Up from the area outside Roger's flat came God. He looked bigger than ever, he must have been eating Red-O-Meat, Hounds Howl for It. Soon he would be a match for a pony. I waved at him, and he peered myopically across the street at me. A double-decker bus lurched towards the request stop by Roger's flat, but it did not slow down although I could see Roger on the crowded platform struggling to jump off. Moving like a sprinting tank, the St Bernard turned in his tracks and charged the bus. The bus came at him like a house on wheels, the driver braking hard. The golden head approached the metal grille. Radiator and God's skull smashed against each other. It seemed evens whether the· bus or the dog would topple. The dog died, but it stopped the bus. I couldn't lift the weight of God alone, but I got his head and chest off the ground, dragged him on to the pavement. Roger was white as that damned detergent. He sat on the pavement. I pulled God past him towards the flat; the blood from the dog's head was soaking into my sleeves. Roger came and helped me with the back legs. In his room he thumbed through a small grey book, then walked to a call-box to phone a vet. I only heard the end of the conversation:

'Yes, my dog's dead. My name's Blester. That's right. Who do I get to take away a dead dog? No, I don't want a special grave or a mausoleum either. I just want a dead dog taken away. I know damn well I'm rude. You can? Thanks, mate. 102a Gladstone Street, basement flat, the door won't be locked. Walk in.'

In the street the conductor was splashing water from a

plastic bucket on the front of the bus. He tried to say something to Roger as we passed. We unlocked the basement door, left God on a plastic macintosh, and got the hell out. Roger left me in the street. He started running very quickly down the pavement, across the road, into a side street. People had to jump out of his way. I sat in a public lavatory to recover. Ford, God and McAllen had liquefied my bowels. I hated the town, I felt unfit for love. Outside I met Devon, walking just in front of his fifty-year-old secretary Elsa, the faint fur of her moustache glinting in the sun.

'You had to leave our little pow-wow in the Unicorn rather suddenly, didn't you, Johnny?'

'I felt sick.'

'Ah ha, out of training for our strong Belston beer.'

Guinness is no stronger in Belston than in Shaftesbury Avenue, but I let it ride.

'Was worried about McAllen.'

'McAllen? Put it out of your mind. It's all over.'

'They haven't hanged him yet. It's not till Saturday morning.'

'Home Secretary's said there won't be a reprieve. In the *Telegraph* this morning, you know.'

'And what's the news with you? What's your latest?'

'I expect you've heard I've been adopted to stand for Belston at the next election.'

'Nobody told me. Which party?'

'Conservative, naturally.'

'You can't tell nowadays, the Labour Party is getting so broad-minded.'

'Ah well, Johnny, I know you're a bit of a red, ha ha, can't count on your vote, can I?'

'I vote in London.'

So the Tories had chosen. I promised myself seriously that I would return to canvass for all his opponents. Elsa stood, tall and muscular like a masseuse, looking at naked dummies in a window. Devon patted her on one wide shoulder-blade, they moved on. Slowly I walked up the hill away from the town.

There was some compass in my head pointing north, to Scotland, which I had never seen, land of soft blended rain, hills and colours. After an hour of slow striding, I looked back into the valley where the sun had set fire to the town, a sun which looked hot enough to crack a pavement, to open fissures for the damned. The damned are the mad; as a baby stretches towards the light, they stretch towards the dark. I found myself in the role of Lot, weeping enough tears in my imagination to form a wife of salt. I would never go back. The Corporation cleaners were all sacked, and the new cleaners in uniforms of flame were sweeping down The Avenue, Mercy Street, Chain Lane, Gladstone Street, Barabbas Street and Palmerston Place. But Sheila was not salt. Then I saw myself as Christian making a pilgrim's egress, not sure whether I was leaving or heading for the golden city, rather looking forward to the Slough of Despond, with one eye on the Delectable Mountains, half-wondering if my woman would follow me. I would probably beat it up in Vanity Fair and settle in its suburbs. I had more in common with Lot, another refugee who didn't know where he was going. Perhaps he set off from the cities of the plain with his leather bag and the juice of the just circulating in his veins, travelling until he came to the first town, without regrets until he found the same old vices marked on unfamiliar faces. One of Ben's nastier rock songs came into my head, 'Pensioner Love':

> You say you're eighty-seven,
> I know you're ninety-three,
> But what the hell's the difference
> Come and crumble with me.
> Uh huh huh, uh huh huh, huh huh huh—
>> Pensioner Love.

I'm a hundred on the surface
But I'm twenty underneath.
I'll bite your neck
If you'll pass my teeth.
Uh huh huh, uh huh huh, huh huh huh—
    Pensioner Love.

Well, sometimes we can and baby
Sometimes we can't.
Let's go out and spend
My disability grant.
Uh huh huh, uh huh huh, huh huh huh—
    Pensioner Love.

As I walked I sang, and as I sang I allowed my mind to
think what it liked. Even these three simultaneous actions
could not satisfy me, I should be doing something for
Western science as well. If I had a plastic track suit I
could have collected my sweat for analysis, or I could
have worn a small bag over my nose and mouth in which
to save my breath, and maybe some toothpaste laboratory
(they wear white coats and hair-cream) would have been
grateful. On the purple-brown of the road the large drops
of rain began. Soon the drops became smaller but thicker
and faster, they were tanning my face pale, doing my
complexion good no doubt, knocking at my left cheek as
if they wanted to come in, till that cheek turned numb
while its twin glowed. The drops diluted the dog blood on
my sleeve, softened the leather of my dusty bag. Because
I was singing the water flopped into my mouth; as my
right foot fell in a puddle the water rose in a clump and
swamped the shoe. Hair drooping with damp, feet and
socks blackening and sliding in their shoes, I was wet to
my pockets.

The first pub I came to was built of a kind of dark-
brown stone I had not seen before. The high sign, hung like
a gallows, read The Stone in the Head. Inside, the bar was
empty, a dank wooden stable. The floor needed sawdust.

103

If it had been comfortable it wouldn't have mattered that it was empty. If it had been friendly the splintering benches would not have bothered me; but the squat, wide-faced woman behind the beer levers was only concerned with her lunch, which was smelling insistently from back-stage, her lunch and her invisible children. Before even summing me up, she was calling to them:

'Harriet, stop doing that to Harry. Now what? Leave the carpet alone then, Harry. It did cost money you know. Now don't—'

'Union Ale, please.'

'—mess around with that liver. You leave it alone or the Toady Man will come for you. I'll ask your father to send for him. Yes I will. I will. He'll go round and say: "There's a naughty, naughty little boy called Harry at the Stone, Mr Toady Man. He needs a good long spell in your hidey place." '

There was a long rhythmic howl.

'Afternoon. I mean morning. Union Ale, please?'

'I'm sorry,' she said angrily. 'Those children, you know, they pester one.'

'Can see that. You have one with me?' Why did she call one child Harry and the other Harriet? Why did the children play so silently yet so wickedly? Order your copy now.

'You have one with me?' I repeated, as she wrenched the top off the high-powered ale.

'Kind,' she said, as if she doubted whether I was kind with rape or theft in mind, 'but I don't think I will. After all, I've got the lunch to cook. And the children.' She turned suddenly, as a dog turns who sees a third cat as the second vanishes into a tree. 'And I'll have the old Toady Man after you too, Howard, if you don't leave yourself alone. Filthy,' she said, turning to me.

'Who's the Toady Man?' Then I wished I hadn't asked, as I saw under my right hand a crudely carved stone toad which had no hole for ash, matches or medicated toothpicks. It was simply a full-time stone image of a toad, its reflection solid in the dull mist of the polished bar. The woman smiled very wide, showing that her back teeth, like mine, were missing.

'You have to keep the children down,' she said. Her head was inclining further and further to one side, looking round some unseen obstacle; she wanted agreement, and her smile got even longer until her face was badly stretched.

'If they're bad we tell them the Toady Man will come and put them in his hidey hole.' I nodded. It didn't mean anything, that nod, it was something to do with my head. She nodded too, towards the stone toad.

'Belonged to my first,' she said. 'He knew all about toads. Box-room full of toad books, toad statues, stuffed toads. Some of them are pretty, all colours. You interested in toads much?'

'I like frogs better.' The ale was dusty and strong in my throat, and the room seemed damp but very hot.

'Funny you should mention frogs,' she said, tapping a pink wart in the centre of her forehead. There was a silence from the room behind the bar.

'Shut up,' she yelled into its darkness.

'Excuse me just a second, you know, I must just . . .'

I bundled through the courtyard to the three-walled Gents. The door stop was a concrete toad with a red jacket. I could see, as I stood there, the other side of the inn sign. It showed a toad, a jewel in the centre of its wide forehead; the stone in the head.

I was back on the road to Scotland and the rain had stopped. Another mile, and sitting on a bench which flaunted a third arm-rest to prevent sleep and copulation among the classes who do not deserve sleep and copulation, I realized that there was nothing about Sheila which I could forget or leave behind so easily. All my skin could recall her gentleness. But I had felt the clouds swelling in the back of my head, I had to get away from people before the rains came down again. I was not afraid of the contentment Sheila had offered so simply, but I was afraid of taking it and then breaking it. From where I sat I could see a telephone box against the sky at the top of the hill, the renewed sun flickering on its panes. The booth smelt of cigars. I phoned Sheila to say I was leaving town. After the initial mechanical noises, clicking, buzzing, came her unmechanical voice:

'Belston 4453.'

'Sheila, I'm leaving town.'

'Hello, this is Belston 4453. Sheila Lewis this end. Is there anybody there? I can't hear you.' I remembered, and pressed Button A.

'Sheila, its Johnny here.'

'What happened to you? I had to eat your lunch.'

'I'm sorry. All sorts of things happened. I met Devon. I went for a long walk.'

'Where are you?'

'On a hill above town.'

'I'm right by the window. Can you see me?'

I shut my eyes. I could see her at the window, she had sashed it high.

'Can I come down to you now?'

'Yes, now.'

'Look, I'm going to be difficult for the next few days. Next few years. Can you manage?'

'Johnny, you're crazy.'

I was off-balance; those words, as she laughed so sweetly, hit me in the throat. My voice went dead and flat.

'Yes, I am, that's right.'

There was a terrible inrush of her breath, a pause, and then she was weeping because of me, two or three miles away at the other end of the line.

'Christ, Johnny, I'm sorry. Please.'

'Difficult. You see what I mean? Difficult.'

Half an hour later we were together. Sheila said:

'You look beat. How much sleep have you been getting? Eat some food, love. I'm going out to get you some presents.' She hugged me. Ten minutes later she was back with a bottle of scotch and some sleeping pills. I couldn't eat. I couldn't focus my mind.

'Will you marry me, Sheila?'

'Wait till you're better and ask me again.'

'Want to ask now.'

'No. Talk about something else. Washing powder or God.'

'Do you believe in God?'

'No. I used to send him messages all the time, but I never got any back. No, I don't.'

'Oh, that's all right then.'

'I'm not going to save you.'

'Yeah. I don't know.'

'Get better. Get well soon.'

We drank to that. The whisky began to work quickly, sending cheerful telegrams down my nerves. I took three pills. Sheila was holding me. Someone had taken off my shoes.

'The taking off of socks,' I said. 'Symbolic. The flat's good, you're good. I take off my socks to you.' But how could I take them off? The removal could be sung heroically:

> With one eye on the sinking solar clock
> The lover smiles, and strips each crimson sock.
> Steam flies his feet, but in his toes remains
> The hot pulsation of his nether veins.
> Sin to a bare-skinned country he is sped,
> He barefoot moves, and bare-faced lies in bed.

Or a high-life motif could creep in: carefully he unrolled his master's stockings from those tapering, aristocratic feet, the envy of half Royal Europe, drawing their silk surface with finesse and the born servant's love of fine craftsmanship over the emblazoned sock-stretchers of the Bourbon King.

Perhaps I should go off on a phony jazz kick: since I was rockin' my cradle on the off-beat I always shed my blue suede bootees when the Pres cut through the airwaves with that groovy tenor. At twenty-six I still went over the top when Lester blew. Tonight he was tooling around 'I Can't Get', and there I was in Heaven Seven, far out as a satellite set alight, while the footskins jived themselves off my dogs.

Or it could be reported in a bulletin like the ones issued when the Queen sneezes: Belston, Thursday. After spending half an uncomfortable day, Mr Johnny Crane this afternoon removed his socks. A spokesman said later that Mr Crane had worn the socks for 'at least thirty-six hours'.

The removal might even lead to a trial scene:

LAWYER: And what was in his socks?

SHEILA: I can't remember.

LAWYER: You can't remember. You can't remember? Can you remember your name?

SHEILA: Sheila.

LAWYER: If you please. Now think back a little, Miss Sheila—I'll assume that is your real name—think back and tell me; don't you recall if there was anything in Mr Crane's socks?

SHEILA: Perhaps some gifts from Santa Claus?

LAWYER: Come come, Miss Sheila. Perhaps this will refresh your memory. I produce Mr Crane, six foot one in his socks.

(*Crane, marked Exhibit* 12a, *is carried in by the Usher, who holds him, feet first, towards witness.*)

SHEILA: I still don't recall . . .

JUDGE: REMEMBER YOU ARE ON OATH.

LAWYER: M'lud, may the Usher remove the Exhibit's socks?

JUDGE: WILL THAT REALLY BE NECESSARY?

LAWYER: It is the only course I can follow, M'lud.

JUDGE: MR USHER, REMOVE THEM.

SHEILA: Ah, now it all comes back to me. Mr Crane's *feet* were in his socks.

LAWYER: If you please.

Sheila must have undressed me, socks included. At first the dreams were warm. Then I was on an arctic

108

expedition. We were on a melting ice-floe, drifting towards temperate England. We had killed and buried one of our comrades on the ice-floe, but his body would not decay. If we threw him in the sea he floated along behind us, drawn by the current which carried us. We buried him in the snow again. He seemed to be retaining a kind of like, like a mammoth in a glacier. The only solution seemed to be to kill more people. We killed more people. Their faces were all familiar to me. Then came good dreams of Sheila, I suppose they were dreams. Then I was in a desert of dead bodies and snakes which fed on them. The dream became funny, it turned into a good dream. With every bad dream I clung closer to Sheila, with every good dream I pressed closer still.

FRIDAY

THE PILLS were very strong and good. Sheila was beside me when I woke at two o'clock, Friday afternoon. My brain was fizzing gently. My body was happy.

'Do you want a doctor, Johnny?'

'I want you.'

'Do you like picnics?'

'I like food anywhere. Is there a sun?'

'I don't know what it is, I didn't have much education, I'm just ignorant, not good enough for you, but there's a big round bright thing in the sky making everything hot.'

'Fine.'

'The basket's ready.'

We caught a bus, which stopped for us where a straight-ranked plantation of young firs marched over the hill and halted smartly at the edge of the road. Immediately we stepped down the sun began to beat through our hair, warming our eyes, overheating our scalps. I carried the basket, Sheila carried an enormous Scottish rug.

Standing on the dry grass by the fence of neat chicken wire, Sheila said:

'It's all fenced in.'

'To keep people out. Why do they make fences so long and straight?'

'Because you can't build crooked fences, the animals would chew down the trees. Later they'll take down the wire and let the trees spread out.'

'You're not ignorant. You know too much.

She stepped over the fence and I followed, the sun shifting like a spotlight to the back of my neck. The grass was wild and tender, climbing high and thin among the small concealing Christmas trees as we wandered towards the centre of the wooden bedroom. Slowly we drifted through the little avenues, singing low and melancholy together, like the hot birds which sail and dive in search of water. Sheila laid down the rug over the soft clumps of grass, and we sat like family picnickers. She opened the basket and I began to unpack the food, jabbering at each item.

'Wine,' I said, 'wine nice as lemonade, the colour of the sun. Wash your hair in it or dab it behind your lobes; the all-purpose wine with silicones. Chicken, sliced from the dead breast, white as light, tender as mud, packed between layers of bread and butter like a fat man in a bed—chicken to cure the ague, plague, humours, vapours, subtle as fine paper, nourishing as a poem.'

'Poetry makes me hungry,' she said. 'Makes me feel dead beat as a simile.'

'Pink fish sandwiches,' I said. 'I love you.'

Her eyes got bigger. 'You don't know me,' she said. 'You don't know me very well.'

'I know I don't. Maybe I will some day. But I know you as well as I know anyone.'

'There's not much to know. After all, I think I'm simple. I love you.'

We pulled off my jacket and ate and drank a little, awkwardly, half in each other's arms, wrapped in the sun. We couldn't tell, as we chewed and gulped, which of us was setting up that slight tremble. We drank the wine, but we didn't peel the fruit; the over-rich cake sat un-sliced and melting as we looked at each other. I knew then that it helped to be out of town. Like warm animals her hands walked over my back as we fell into a kiss. She counted the buttons of my shirt aloud as she undid them carefully, and my fingers inefficiently opened her blouse

112

and smoothed it away from her white shoulders. We were promising promises and smiling as we undressed ourselves quickly without standing up, a laughable manœuvre, until we lay at last open to every shift in the air and each other's bodies. Her large breasts moved under my chest, for long seconds our thighs kept their distance, then suddenly, simultaneously joined as our kiss deepened. We were moving slowly into the wood again, but this time an undisciplined, hotter wood, where the birds and their songs were twice the size and the ground was swaying under our hips. Her lips fell away and she said:

'I believe in reafforestation, it is an essential amenity,' so that we earthquaked in laughter and the kiss we returned to was shaken with laughter. I opened my eyes and caught her looking at me, and we both laughed again as my hand cruised from her neck to her right breast, returning to its home. I could not think for love, only that if Sheila were ever harmed I would be killed; and then we were laughing again, and on we glided until we were spinning down together through that expanding bright sky, like a lark after his song, down to that rug, the tartan of some minor clan. We lit cigarettes, blowing the slight smoke at the trees, over our bodies, playing like children because we loved each other. The sun had began to cool as we made love once more, cocooned in that Scottish pattern, quietly this time, a small planet circling a permanent, invisible sun, whispering our own musical nonsense. We asked no questions, gave no answers on that lazy island in the trees. Progressively, as it became colder, we dressed.

'Come to the ball tonight, love,' I said.

'Man, I need some sleep. I love you, but I need sleep.'

'But we slept nearly twenty-four hours.'

'You were talking and dreaming, you trouble-maker. I couldn't sleep at all. You go to the ball, I'll sleep. Some day we must get our sleep synchronized.'

'I promised my sister I'd go.' Sheila laughed. 'It's true, I'm taking my sister Joan.'

'Well, all right then.'

Back at Sheila's, I rang Joan's flat and arranged to meet her at The Most, a cocktail-bar dedicated to the Americans and a poor selection of jazz records by a young landlord who was with it but was losing a lot of money. It was getting late. While I changed, Sheila ran a bath. A draught turned my legs even whiter than usual as I tried and failed to find my braces. It was an east wind, probably from long-suffering China. I used to have a pair of braces with leather thongs badly worn, elastic frayed and nearly gone, they were my own, my braces. McAllen must be sitting in his stone box with two warders but no braces or belt, just to be on the safe side of suicide. How did he keep his trousers up? Perhaps he did not mind any more if they fell down. Sitting down to think that one out, I could see through the window a short old woman in a silky dress with more colours than I could count, moving along the street out of the wind, looking about her for some late baby to smile at or dog to pat. She didn't look up, but I smiled at her; she looked beautiful, wearing that tailored rainbow, and a sunset was beginning at the end of the street. Hers was a dress designed to delight children, to teach them all the colours easily. She had lived through more wars than I had.

A young man, his young wife and their black-haired, kicking, carried child came out of a house and kissed the old woman. Each touched the nape of her unthreatened neck. The small boy she took closest to her, and her feet moved in a quarter circle and back in a miniature dance. I wanted them to sit, defying Belston custom, all on the doorstep to play with that child, but they moved indoors. As the old woman walked into the house, she paused and smiled down the street, especially at the sunset. Quite coincidentally, the street stopped roaring for a moment. From the direction of London I could hear the droning grief of the mother of McAllen as she tucked his son in a second-hand cot and shut the window to cut off the noise and dirt of the trains. In the kitchen her kettle was boiling dry, and steam drops gathered on the low ceiling.

I dragged my trousers over my waist and used an elastic

belt. Next I organized my pockets. I remembered Ford's knife and pushed it inside my heavy-shouldered dinner-jacket so that I could throw it away somewhere. From seventeen handkerchiefs I chose a white one the size of a suburban lawn. About twenty pounds went into my left trouser pocket. Into the jacket went a packet of ten cigarettes in hygienic Cellophane, a packet of twenty with three left, and a packet of ten with four left. One packet contained the kind that sailors smoke, another held snouts for lovers, and the third had long mentholated fags, they burn your throat and cool it in the same drag. I lack brand loyalty. I added a book of matches, less bulky than a box, and I would advise all dandies to follow my example. I thought that a quarter bottle of scotch might fit, but it made me look deformed. Also, I remembered that I should stay sober, or in some condition like sober. I left the drink for Sheila. The dance invitation nestled in beside the knife. I took out the knife and looked at it. It was heavy, but delicately balanced. Should you hold it with your knuckles uppermost? That was wrong; it limited the movement of my wrist to a direct, maybe deadly stab. Nobody wants that kind of unpleasantness, not in England. I threw the knife down and it jagged automatically into the lino, shivering until I picked it up, pressed back the blade and dropped it into my pocket. I smoothed my shirt, and for the final touch of Brummel, clipped on my tie. I kissed Sheila as she dozed pinkly in her bath, slung my limp mack over my shoulder and tried to saunter nonchalantly out of the flat. First thing I tripped over the doormat. My mack was a nuisance, so I threw it back in the flat.

In front of me on top of the bus sat a short-haired man on his way home from the Market, where the pubs are open all day on Fridays. He was explaining himself to two cheery middle-aged women two rows in front of him.

'I am not afraid of any bloody man. All my mates were slaughtered in the bloody war, but they think they won the war sitting on their bloody arses. Well, look, I'll tell you, only one man ever made me afraid, he was a bloody

German not a bloody Englishman. He had a rifle and I had a rifle, and I bloody well shot first. I'm not scared of any bloody man. I tell you the Germans are the best bloody fighters in the world. I should know, I've had experience.'

The woman laughed and the fatter one said: 'What would you do if you met Robin Hood—'

'I'm not scared of any bloody man—'

'—and he had his bow and arrow?'

'Oh, oh yes, well, you—'

'You'd run in the woods, that's what you'd do. And what would you do if you met Davy Crockett?'

'I tell you this: I only been scared of one bloody man in my life, and he was a German, not a bloody Englishman. I was a bloody infantryman.'

'Why did we win the war if the Germans were so good at fighting?'

'Well.'

The second woman joined in indignantly: 'They would have won if they'd been better than us.'

'I don't know,' said the man, so I joined in for him.

'We had Walt Disney on our side,' I said.

'What?' said the fatter woman.

'Bloody Donald Duck,' said the man whose mates were slaughtered in the bloody war. As I got off the bus the fatter woman was angry.

'Aren't you proud of being English?' she asked the man.

'I'm proud of being alive,' he said.

It was only nine, but Joan was early, wrapped in a dress the colour of a billiards-table cloth, graceful as a long-legged bird, on the tallest stool in The Most, laying down political theory to a stringy dress designer. He seemed chatty, turning to me and asking: 'Who would you like to see as Prime Minister?'

'Johnny Dankworth,' I said. 'Or Fidel Castro, with Michael Foot blowing Foreign Secretary.'

'Seriously.'

'Seriously. Gaitskell may be at shorter odds. But he once spent a lot of energy denying that he ever said that he didn't trust Macmillan. I haven't trusted him too far since then. And look how he digs the bomb.'

'You grant he's sincere?'

'I don't grant that people are sincere without proof. Everyone seems to grant sincerity to people they don't like, as a small charity to show that fair play is uppermost. Liberace, they say, is sincere. Godfrey Winn, sincere as they come. Billy Graham, the most sincere. Even Devon, they tell me he's sincere. Why should he be? What's in sincerity for him? He's sincere about money. I don't know what Gaitskell's sincere about.'

Joan stared at the ceiling. It was covered with a Venetian-style painting of the canonization of Charlie Parker. Charlie Christian took up one corner; he was blowing electric harp. Fats Waller was sinking into the piano stool of an outsize cloud. One of Buddy Bolden's feet was visible, on it was tattooed 'Buddy Bolden'. Gabriel, holding his horn abjectly behind his back, was carrying out the ceremony. I remembered all my money.

'Joan, we're going to eat well tonight. I got twenty pounds on me.'

'Brother,' she said.

'Yes, my sister,' I said, like a translation from the Chinese. 'Real food tonight, now.'

We left the man to design some dresses and crossed the road to the International Hotel. Electric chandeliers and tasselled awnings in crimson set the stage for an Edwardian fairy-tale. The menu came on a scroll, so that you had to unroll it and pin it down with salt, pepper and several kinds of mustard—French, English, crusted in a crystal jar or fresh in a tube. We bit into long whisky cocktails afloat with small icebergs, ice that rang loud in an un-flawed empty glass so that the wine waiter could hear you finish. At the table behind us sat the Mayor with his official party. They seemed to be half way through a seance. Way to the right stood piano, bass and drums, waiting for Ben's trio. We ate so many light dishes designed as appetizers that we were full by the time the main course arrived. At the International they take the labour out of eating; they cut the fat off the meat and the bones out of sardines. Baked beans are peeled before serving.

'What are you going to do about Ford?' asked Joan.

'When did you see him? I didn't know you knew he was around.'

'I've seen him almost every week for the last three months,' she said. 'I didn't tell you he was around because I thought he'd bother you too.'

'Well, he bothers me. But he's my brother.'

'He said you helped him. There I was sitting at my typewriter last night, trying to work out the right skirt-length for Belston in the evening, and Ford had to phone from London to say how wonderful you'd been. You know —nobody never done nothing like that for me before, till you're down you don't know what your friends are made of, all that stuff. The week before last he was cursing you, but now—'

'What was he cursing me about?'

'Oh, you know, for being the favourite, for having the luck, for being the great blues singer—'

'—Ford thinks that?'

'So do I. I know you have bad nights sometimes, but you can sing, anyway. Even if you have problems, anyone who listens to you sing isn't going to worry themselves about your problems, they're going to pray for their sons to have voices like yours. I am no sucker for singers, Johnny. But when you sing the people hang on to each other as if they're on the Big Dipper at a fair. It's like a Welsh preacher acting out the story of Job. Great singer. When I lent you that two hundred pounds it was an investment in your voice, not charity. End of press release.'

'Did Ford sound happy?'

'Yes, but he wants more help, no, not more money and not just a tuning-fork. He wants you to help him sing.'

'I shan't be in London much.'

'He'll travel for lessons. He doesn't trust voice teachers, but he trusts a singer.' Her answer was so quick that I knew this was what she wanted from me, Ford had asked her for this. I needed to be carried half the time, and here was Ford hitching a piggy-back from me.

'Let him ask me and I'll do it,' I said. But I wasn't thinking so much about Ford, I was thinking about my own voice, how I could let it fly out at any time like a steel-winged brown bird. A voice that could run round a hall in an eightieth of a second, interfering with everyone. Three men in black and white bowed from the band's little platform in the corner. The drums began to patter on their lonely way, a slight eccentric and relaxed beat. The cymbal work was delicate, like a field-mouse scratching at a golden gong. The bass plodded in, changed its slow mood and sprinted quietly alongside the drums. In burst the piano with all ten fingers, there was Ben knocking out the first chorus of 'If You See Me Comin' '. His hands hesitated, jumped, then only his right hand was operating, tickling out the melody as his left hand beckoned me. Ben pushed up the mike for me and I let them have the blues:

'If you see me comin', sash your window high,
  Now if you see me comin', sash your window high.
  And if you see me goin'—hang your head and cry.'

The manager was shifting from foot to foot. Again I was happy, they would have to tear down the hotel before I stopped. I made up verses: 'I'll tell you what I'm going to do,' I shouted. 'Now listen:

'I'll buy a top-hat from Blooter's, walk down Gladstone Street,
  I'll nail that hat to my head and I'll walk down Gladstone Street,
  And I'll take off my hat to every honest man I meet.

119

'Well, these women in Belston, they are as cold as ice,
All the Belston women are cold as frozen ice,
If you want to lay them, you have to ask them twice.

'I've seen a thousand kettles, not one of them was white.
Seen a thousand pots and kettles, not one of them was
white.
I've met a thousand women, not one would treat me
right.

'When the grass is red and the snow is pink and blue,
When the grass grows red and the snow falls pink and
blue,
Start brewin' coffee, I'll be comin' back to you.

'So if you see me comin', well, sash your window high,
Now if you see me comin', sash your window high,
And if you see me goin'—hang your head and cry.'

Ben was laughing, a very good sign. He looked up at me:
'You seem to be dressed in something,' he said.
'They call it a dinner-jacket,' I said. 'All the best slobs
are wearing them. They tell me tails are going out.'
'That's evolution, man. You going to this ball tonight?'
'Sure. You're not playing there too?'
'We're not on the bill, but the relief group cancelled,
so here we are. The relief relief trio straight from a strip
Khartoum. Meet Bob Blackburn.'
We made gestures at each other. He looked young
enough to be my son, but he really managed that bass,
which looked old enough to be his grandfather.
'And this is Flak Peters. They say Art Blakey can make
drums talk, but Flak makes them scream.' I knew old
Flak. He made his musical name with big radio bands
after the war. In the war he made his name by flying a
Blenheim and telling his gunner to come in on the off-beat.
After the plane was shot up by an anti-aircraft gun on the
French coast, it limped back to England, where Peters lay

120

in hospital half-conscious for three weeks, drumming silently with his fingers on the sheet. Then his gunner asked if he remembered what happened.

'It was the flak, Jack,' he answered. This pleased him so much that he turned the phrase into a jazz riff, chanting it to himself at intervals. He stopped only after dictating a letter to Duke Ellington, offering the sentence as the title for a composition. Since then everyone called him Flak.

'See you, then,' I said vaguely. Ben tossed me half a crown for singing and I returned to Joan.

'You can sing,' she said. We dug into a soggy thing which had been soaked in liqueur. A man tried to sell me cigars. Another brought the bill, another brought the wine bill. Someone brought my coat, I told him I didn't bring a coat. The manager tiptoed over to ask how we enjoyed the meal and to thank me for singing. I didn't tip him, I know my way around. Joan went to the Ladies to clean up, she had got very dirty eating that meal.

The Town Hall had been decorated with taste and discretion. Things had probably been planned by a man in the City Architect's Office called Theat, who thought the sun vulgar. So the building wore an apologetic jumble-sale air of celebration, though of course its innate dignity as the principal civic building was not impaired. A semi-sacred building, it is an amenity. Like a tree, a canal, a slipper bath, an El Greco, a public lavatory—an amenity to be preserved.

As flunkies closed in, I had to explain again that I had no coat. Perhaps because of all the excitement, Joan went to the Ladies again after we arranged to split up and meet for a drink later. No one was dancing well, but the dance was coasting along, moving downhill perhaps, but moving. Major Desert was drunk already. Secretaries in flowered dresses formed a herbaceous border down one side of the floor. There were faint signs of syncopation as the band began the Beguine. The bass player was improvising. Not only was this tinge of jungle wilderness creeping into the music, but a large councillor was tapping his foot in time

121

while he told jokes by the bar. I took a large scotch and listened to him. It went like this.

Joke One: 'Now, well, there was this man, you see, there was this man, and he got married to a woman juggler you see, very common woman, very common indeed. And one day she said to him: "How about you coming into the act?" you see, and so he said: "Well, that sounds all right—" ' At that point Joan signalled to me, so I fetched her a drink, which says little for the man she was talking to, Mr Verdun, something in transport. I left them after saying 'Mr Verdun,' because I couldn't think of anything else to say. I got back in time for the end of

Joke Two: 'So he turned it upside down, you see. Then the tiger came downstairs, looked at it, sniffed and went off. The elephant came downstairs, sniffed it and walked out. The bull came down, took one look at it and left. Finally the rabbit came down. He looked at it. He sniffed it. Then he gobbled it up and ran upstairs again.'

There was a break of laughter from the audience as Roger, gloomily serving at the bar, refuelled my glass, but this councillor kept a straight face as he whipped into his third, one I had heard before.

Joke Three: 'A woman went to see her doctor, you see, and he happened to be asleep when she came into the room. Well, the woman looked round the room and the first thing she noticed was a boy standing in the corner with a telephone on his head. So she—'

Somebody's hand jumped on to my shoulder and held it firmly. When I turned, I was looking into an entirely new face, a middle-aged bit of a man with dark hair as smooth as a Labrador's.

'Hello, Johnny, how are you these days?'

'Sorry, look, I'm sure I ought to remember a name like yours. Your face seems—but—'

'Never mind, never mind. Gerry Dunne, used to write about you.'

I knew the name all right, but he had grown a wig, this jazz critic turned impresario. He once compared me to the

122

seventh best blues shouter in the States, but then he thought the seventh best blues shouter was very special.

'Of course. But I haven't seen you in years. Thanks for writing about me.'

'That was three years ago, you sound better than ever now. I dined at the International.'

'That was fun,' I said. 'But I do better than that. Three years ago I was a mess. That was a long time ago. Why, in those days you could go up West, buy a gallon of porter, a firkin of best King Edward baccy, the Royal Box at the Tivoli, a night at the Ritz with Marie Lloyd and five acres of slum property, and still have change out of a ninepenny bit.'

'Like to hear you again.' He said that as if he believed he had heard me at my peak.

'I'll fix it. There's a piano in the band room and I can borrow a pianist.'

'Forgotten, Johnny? I play piano.' Forgotten, Johnny? Bandleaders wrote songs about the way Dunne treated a piano. Squarer than an Oxo cube.

'Fine. This way.'

'How's your range?'

'I'm higher up than I ever knew about before, and I still get good and low.'

He fiddled with the piano. I hummed a melody, and the fourth time he caught enough of it, plunked four chords and in we went. It was a slow little poem by Ben called 'Blue Spring'. I made it mellow:

'A man sits counting the days of spring,
  His heart may tremble but his mind won't stir,
  And one thought runs through all his waking—
  I would have burnt my heart for her.

'If she had recognized my voice,
  Or called my name, or listened to me sing,
  I would have left the careless human race
  For one hour of her careful loving.

123

'When spring swings round again, and I am here,
I will forget the terrors of her voice.
But I would stay with terror at my ear
And burn my heart, if I had any choice.'

Second time through I gave the ballad all the slow tricks, my voice swinging like a pendulum. He was shaken, I could see that, he hadn't expected anything like that. Next we rolled into a hearty old hate-the-world-and-you-most-of-all-baby blues. He was happier, his fingers bouncing now in familiar territory. By the end he was excited, behaving like a live audience, while his cigarette toasted itself brown in the ashtray. Something was still wrong though, he kept glancing at the corner of the room, expecting my ten-foot bodyguard to be standing there with a Sten-gun and a grin. Even his excitement was mixed with something else, under the control of some thoughtful plan. He smiled. I don't like the regimental, similar shine of perfect teeth, maybe I envy them. But the smile was not designed to frighten me. Dunne was amused by some silent memo he had written in his mind. He shut down his smile to speak:

'Let's get some drinks.' That was a good thing to say, I can appreciate good talk. I wanted to ask what his secret was and accept a drink at the same time; his face was obscure and slick as the numberless plastic stopped clock on the wall beyond his shoulder.

'Thanks,' I said, 'this is nice whisky. But there's one thing: what are you thinking about at the back of your head all the time?'

'Sheila Lewis,' he said after no pause at all. I felt myself breathing in.

'She sings well,' I said. There was no need to make a speech. I was Sheila's lover, not her agent.

'I'll tell you. I think she sings so well I want her for a series of jazz shows touring round the country, then maybe abroad. Broadcasts too.'

124

'That's why you're in Belston. Who else would be travelling?'

He told me, a good list including Ben's trio and five regular British poll-winners. My shoes were black, polished and soft. Bending over them, I twitched first my left big toe, then my right, then both together. The leather responded to the twitches and one by one and then both together my shoes winked at me. Any pleasure I got from this operation was small change, it was only just on the right side of the line between debit and credit, boredom and enjoyment. The only reason that it granted even such a faint kick was that my big toes twitched in strict rhythm, then each padded back to its appointed place in line.

'What does Sheila say?'

'She was funny about it. Odd, I mean. Still, it might work out.'

'More, Mr Dunne.'

'Gerry.'

'More please, Gerry.'

'She said she'd have to talk to you.'

'I don't own Sheila.'

'Johnny, I'll be fair and open. I thought your voice was still somewhere in the second row, that's how I recalled it. Sheila wouldn't make up her mind until I'd heard you sing. Now I know why. I think you could fit in the show with Sheila.'

'Contracts? Duets?'

'Right.'

'Gerry, here is my right hand. If you can use it, chop it off.'

He dropped his voice. I knew there was a catch.

'Johnny, I hear you are—and let me finish—a little unstable. Not your fault, of course, but the buzz is that you're—unreliable. That's the only snag.'

'I can sing,' I said. 'No matter how upset I am, I can always sing. When I can't write my name or even remember my name, I can sing. Put in a huge breakdown clause if

125

you like, you won't have to use it. I can sing through tears
better than Judy Garland.'

He looked at me, and now, though it was the same
smile, I didn't find it mechanical.

'All right, we'll risk it. Right? Why not ring Sheila?'
He waited outside the wooden booth, scratching its scratched
surface with a neatly rounded fingernail.

'Now this character Dunne,' I told her, 'and don't hit
me if you've heard this one before—'

'Johnny, I'm not going on his crummy tour.'

'Listen, listen, listen. What do you mean?'

'Honey, I want to be with you. I don't know if I've
adopted you or you've adopted me. There it is. That's all.'

'Listen, love,' I said. 'Suddenly it's fairyland. The old
witch is dead. I'm coming on the tour too.'

She made the sound effects of happiness. 'Come back
soon,' she said. 'I'll be at our flat.'

'I want to sing with Ben, but I'll be back.'

As I put it down, the blackness of the receiver brought
back McAllen. Dunne and I settled plans over big whiskies.
He had to drive back to London, so I wandered away
down the panelled corridor. Orange net skirts brushed
against dusty radiators. The door of the Mayor's Parlour
was open and I glimpsed the back of Joan's billiards dress.
She was on business, writing the caption for a photograph. In his suit of soiled brown paper the photographer
leant against an immemorial table under the portraits
of mayors, most of them looking like Richard II or Richard
III, and recorded an important group.

Before him as he muttered 'Now, will you all move.
Closer together, please, closer I said. Haven't got a wide-
angle lens, can't afford one. No, lady, over there, over
there. Try and look at me as if I was Tony Curtis. Now.
Just one more,' stood seven people in a formal semicircle,
rubbing shoulders. Their background was a door which
needed a wash, surmounted by a geometrical wooden
carving of a rising or setting sun. All seven looked alert,
if nothing else, and reading from left to right they were

disgusted, sagging, sturdily dumb, steel-hearted, faded, prettily drunk, and camera-happy. All stared blankly into the camera as the flash illuminated their stalwart postures (i.e. standing up).

On the left was the Town Clerk, disgusted because he did not like dances, perhaps a reasonable view in the circumstances, and the more so because he does not drink. Next to him, the lady chairman of the Education Committee, with the saddest eyes in the world, sagging because the schools were rotting and she knew it all the time, but next week she would present a bright picture of Education in Belston and take an economy cut like an adult taking medicine. The came the Mayor, a marble-fleshed masterpiece, a civic ornament, playing with his chins like a baby with a rattle. In the Grand Raffle he had won four prizes, including an alarm clock which would be useful if he ever had to work in the morning. Having just accepted, after protesting, another two hundred and fifty pounds rise from the Council, he was delighted with the tin clock, which has a large round face like his own, only with Roman numerals smeared with paint which takes in light by day and lets it out at night. The bell, mounted on top, had a painful vibration. I know; Ford broke mine. It cost £1 16s. 4d.

Winning a 14 lb. cake, it was announced later, he generously auctioned it, and it raised £4 8s. for the Old People's Church Fund, being sold to a lady who will keep it in her front window because of pride. Her name is Mrs Charranisse of Whirly Way, and her nose falls like a half-melted candle towards her chin. She keeps birds in cages and gets prizes for it, as she should, for she keeps the breeds pure and pays a great deal of money for each bird. She makes sure they do not escape into the dangerous sky. They are so bright they would be pecked out of the air if they ever flew away from Whirly Way. But they do not fly very well. One of them says Humpty Dumpty. Mrs Charranisse buys them from a moaning man who steals sacks from the Corporation, which can spare them. These his aunt sews into overcoats. He gets very cold in winter.

Next to the Mayor stood the Chief Constable, wearing Himmler spectacles. He retires next year if they don't find out about him before then. He believes in punishment of all sorts, for everyone. By simply standing there he summed up all that is wrong in the relations between the police and the public. Somewhere in Belston, if you believe in the sportsmanship of nature, there must have been his complement—a round Rubens of a bobby with a scarlet nose to match his cheeks, big soft hands and big hard feet, jocular pursuer of small boys who bathe in reservoirs, finger-wagging foe of masked burglars carrying bags marked Swag, proceeder and apprehender, nanny-shadower and cook-tickler—but if there was I had never seen him.

Next came Mrs Charranisse, whom we all know and love, and then the Mayor's wife, tall, graceful, her hair dark as boots, round-breasted, tipsy and pretty. Torn between secretaryship and modelling at the age of twenty-two, she married the Mayor, who was fifty in those days. Two years later she ran away, and returned three weeks later, smiling to herself. I went drinking with her a few times. I smiled at the Mayor, silently asking his permission to smile at his wife. His mouth moved upwards, so I smiled at her. Beside her, pleased to be photographed, was Devon. He was so pleased that his smile was genuine. In front of him he held an honest-to-goodness pipe. After the third flash the photographer bundled up his gear, but the Mayor held up a pale hand.

'You must all take a drink with me. I insist.'

A flunky, on cue, paraded in with a tray of drinks. He wore a green thing which might have been traditional Sexagesima Sunday wear for Belston peasants. I found out by sniffing which glasses were sherry and which were whisky.

'This is my brother, Johnny Crane,' said Joan to everybody. 'He's in town for the revue at the Acorn.'

'Yes,' said the Mayor.

'Oh yes,' said the Mayoress, as she rubbed her right hand in among that sooty hair. 'Hello, Johnny. Don't see

128

much of you these days. Golly, you sang beautifully at that place tonight.' She gave me an obvious smile. She said: 'He's very witty and such a wonderful singer. You know he sings like a demon. I mean that nicely. Like a man possessed. He sings so well.'

Holding a drink in each hand, she shook her head and gave a big sigh. One of the drinks flopped about in its glass, splashing the front of her dress. She looked as if she wanted me to mop it off her. The Chief Constable looked baffled, then coughed.

'So you're an actor,' he cross-examined. He looked as if he knew all about actors, but I couldn't see his eyes behind those spectacles, the lenses reflected the light like polished steel. Mrs Charranisse giggled like a cage bird, the Education lady gave a smile of depression, and the Town Clerk nodded slowly, three times. This annoyed me terribly.

'Why did you nod three times slowly at me?' I asked quietly.

Everyone blinked at the same time. The Town Clerk pursed his lips and went on pursing them and staring through me, so I asked:

'Why are you pursing your lips? Why stare through me?'

I wasn't annoyed by now; if anything, I was scared. It seemed he could no longer bring himself to look at me. He turned his gaze to Mrs Charranisse.

'Perhaps we ought to dance,' he said glumly, and thumped out without looking at me.

The Mayoress had the Chief Constable on one arm and Devon on the other, but she twisted her head round and faced me: 'I think we ought to dance,' she said. 'For old times' sake.'

'Come along, dearest,' said the Mayor flatly. Joan and I had the tray of drinks to ourselves.

'What's the matter with that old Town Clerk?' I asked.

'He broke his hearing aid,' said Joan. 'He's deaf.'

There was somebody white standing at my shoulder. It was the bust of a grimy dignitary. The marble reminded me of days when the sky is one great cloud. All the grooves of the carved face sheltered deposits of grit, in one lay a straight grey hair. Marble busts at least do not waste as much marble as monuments involving sculptured lounge suits. Busts of composers are busts simply because busts are more functional than statues, sawn off at the shoulders, the great men can stand as solid guardians on the grandeur piano. 'Buy Beethoven,' they seem to say, 'Make Mine Mozart.' I decided to cast a plastic bust of Thelonious Monk with a real coolie hat for Ben's piano. Monk among the pianists is a helicopter among jets. As I left Joan to scribble names in her notebook, Tom approached, walking methodically, using his left foot first, then his right, then his left again.

Tom said: 'Watch his hands.'

He nodded at three women standing in line in front of Devon. One was Devon's secretary, so she had to stand there. Devon's hands were palm upwards, side by side, about six inches from his cummerbund. They jumped apart, then flicked as he shrugged his shoulders. Slowly, left hand approached right hand, covered it gently for a moment, grabbed it and twisted it over viciously. The hands wrestled. They unlocked, and right hand became a fist to strike three times the open left. It was part hand jive, part judo.

'It's a stock exchange,' I said. 'My stock goes up because I'm here. So does yours. We must maintain the prestige essential to our status as great powers.' I could see McAllen leaning over the balcony, he was stroking his face. It looked like McAllen. Velma's chin dropped on my shoulder.

'You going to sing tonight, Johnny?'

'Sing about what?'

'Sing about song.'

'Tonight. What am I meant to say? Tonight. You know McAllen?'

'I know about McAllen.'

'He's being hung. Not tonight. In the morning.'

130

'You ought to give up thinking. Not that you do think. You feel your way around,' said Tom.

'Drink, don't think,' said Velma, curling an arm round my waist. 'Was my low-cut number all right, Tom? At rehearsal?'

'You'll be fine. Maybe more attack. Friendly persuasion is nice, but you have to hit an audience.'

As we danced away from him, Velma, closing in with every step, said: 'What do you think of the world, Johnny?

'You want to know what I think of the world? I'm very glad you ask me that. The world needs a wash. If the world swings, it swings on rusty hinges, will soon fall off. I do not think the world is made of worms. No, the world is a papier-mâché of pound notes. The world is not round. It is not even like an orange, flat at both ends, though I have yet to see an orange flat at both ends. The world is badly bent.'

Roger's pet pupil speaking. Velma snuggled, the world looked less bent, but when I was with Sheila the world seemed nearly round. To dance reasonably with Velma is impossible. Her feet are clever, the rest of her is plain irresponsible; her surroundings blur into soft lights whenever she lowers those curving eyelids. A partner has three choices: he can stay at arm's length and think about Oliver Cromwell; he can sway with the tidal body of Velma until he becomes too uncomfortable; or he can take her home quickly. I compromised, thinking about Sheila and talking continuously about the revue. Velma needs more than one man, a passionate Co-operative Society. She always seems happy.

'What's wrong with you? Is it McAllen again?' she asked me, and I had to stop in mid-anecdote. Sheila wouldn't have to ask.

'I love Sheila.'

'Christ, I know that. Everybody knows that.'

'Does Devon know?' There was no reason why Devon shouldn't know, but the less he knew about me, the better I liked it. Whisky was rising in a dark gold fog to my head.

'Your face is red and white, Johnny, you better sit down.'

I stepped back and held her hands, as I had done in *Much Ado About Nothing.*

'I'd better go and sit down,' I said. 'Your body is white and red. I love you a bit, Velma, but I love Sheila.'

'Break my heart and I won't buy your records. Sheila is welcome.' So we kissed each other and she danced with Tom. I carried from the bar a halved sun of whisky. Wishing to contemplate it in peace, I took it to the Mayor's Parlour and sat in a leather armchair whose arms came as high as my shoulders. Laughter trickled out of my mouth, but dried as I saw Devon and his secretary considering me. He sent her on some errand and joined me with an endearing chuckle—if you are easily endeared. On the far side of a long, heavyweight table he sat facing me.

'And how are you enjoying yourself, Johnny? Glass full, I see. Nice for you young people, you can relax. Manage to bring Miss Lewis? Never mind. You're lucky, I've had to talk business most of the evening.'

'What business is that?'

'More TV.' He made a little television gesture. 'Another series of Great Murders Through the Ages. Dramatized documentaries, probably not quite your cup of tea, Johnny, not quite your cup of tea.'

'Good entertainment, though?'

'Certainly.'

'Do you hate murderers?'

'No, no, you don't understand me at all, Johnny. I don't hate murderers, I hate their crimes, the things they stand for.'

'Then why this hanging?'

'Because it must be. Perhaps I sound old-fashioned to you, but I believe that murder must be duly and sufficiently punished. Punishment is needed, and there is only one just punishment for killing.'

Devon was reddening. I felt flat as a desert. Then a wind began to rise, stirring up the sand in me, stinging sand. His face was a roc's egg, a great pink shell, an Easter egg or a trick egg. What happened inside that shell, what gluey yolk hardened there into small bones, what would be the next bird of a thought to break from that incubated head? Another vulture? The egg watched me. Then I saw it was no egg, but a boulder which could roll down the slope to crush me. Nothing would be born from it. But in its fissures bred six-legged, armoured, poisonous insects in lovable furry costumes. Trying to break the spell of that head, I tried to see it not as a stone but as a head, I tried to see those two small, close fossils as ears, those blue-and-white flaws as eyes. If they were ears they were not listening. If they were eyes they were not looking. A black and scarlet cavity opened in the stone and Devon spoke his words weightily. They dropped like stones at a stoning.

'Johnny,' he said, 'without faith how can you understand capital punishment? I don't claim to speak for any church or even most Christians, but I have thought about this a great deal, and although what I am going to say may appear simple to the point of absurdity, yet I want you to understand that it is my true belief. All great truths, they say, are simple. You see, I know, I know there is an after-life, and we will all be punished there. Maybe you think some innocent people have been hanged, or partly guilty people have been executed unjustly. That's an old argument, but I won't give you the old answers. I believe that such people, if any there be, have their recompense in Heaven.'

My head hurt. For the first time in my adult life I believed that Devon was talking sincerely.

'There are far more terrible ways to die, you know, Johnny. By fire, by strangling with the hands, by the knife. The murderer at least has every opportunity for repentance. How many of us are granted that much? Jesus drove the money-lenders from the Temple with a scourge—'

(I didn't read the book, but I saw the picture.)

'—Jesus believed in punishment. He chose to be executed

133

himself. Could he have done that if capital punishment itself were evil?'

It was a drunk's argument, but I was drunk as well.

'Take this murderer McAllen,' he said, laying at last his fingers on that poor sod's neck. 'He killed a fellow creature. He thought he could get away with it—but he didn't.' Devon grinned. 'Sometimes our policemen really are wonderful. Anyway, seriously, he must now be punished, he must pay, he must be punished, he must hang.' He looked at his watch.

When he looked up from that watch a second later I was leaning across the table, holding Ford's knife and making a noise with my mouth. I didn't know where to stab him, but I wanted badly to stab him. Maybe in the tongue. Merely by leaning backwards in his chair he was out of reach. I rounded the table, but it was too late, I cooled, I wasn't going to touch him now. Without looking, knowing I had lost, I turned back to my chair and wept. He could have watched safely, but he backed out, the winner. I had cast Ford as Cain, myself as Abel. That was bad miscasting, I would never try that again. With my knife I stabbed hard at my left hand. My eyes hurt, but the wound made by the knife did not hurt much at the time. I wiped my eyes, put the knife in my pocket, tied up my hand with my handkerchief. What would I spoil next?

I climbed through the window on to the fire escape and up to the roof. If they wanted to find me they could follow the blood which dropped from my hand. The tarred roof was flat and springy. I ambled by battlements until I came to a forty-five-degree slope with a drainpipe running up it to a small turret with a platform and a flagpole. There was no apparent danger in the climb, the furthest I could slip back to the main roof was twenty feet, but I pretended this was heroic and convinced myself I must reach the platform.

I only had to drag my body, which seemed heavier than usual, up the drainpipe to the top and then step into the turret. The first part took me two attempts, mainly because I wanted to try sliding down the slates. Becoming dizzy, I lay in the cool of the turret, peering through those virgin battlements to the black and yellow street. People were beginning to leave, howling for taxis or tripping away on inaudible feet. The dresses of girls were pale in the murk. A padlocked box beside the flagpole presumably contained the Union Jack; but I should raise my own banner. What could I use? I needed my trousers, so it had to be the handkerchief, still gently dripping. But I had lost my encounter with Devon so unmistakably that the blood was not to my credit, it was a sign of surrender to violence, and I still was not finally defeated. To signal the reverse I could have raised the Union Jack with a few spots of blood painted on the white stripes, but now I wanted to make no concessions—energetic despair was the mood. So I clicked open Ford's knife. The wood of the flagpole was thick and hard. It took twenty minutes to cut it down. I laid it carefully on the platform, then almost fell for fright when I saw a short, silent man astride a battlement behind me. Seated like that at such a height it could only be Roger.

'I came up to cut down the flagpole,' he said. 'Have you seen it?'

'I cannot tell a lie. I done it with me little shiv.'

Roger looked at the stars as if wondering what unpleasantness was going on up there.

'You won't get away with this, actor. First you insult Devon when I was stalking him. Then you cut down my flagpole. It's not on, Crane, its just not on.'

He evidently hated me less than most people. But what gave him the right to hate everyone, to let Elspeth bear his child by herself?

'What have you done for Elspeth?'

He faced me with closed eyes and joined his hands behind his head. The carnation in the buttonhole of his white barman's jacket looked as though it had never been alive.

'More than you, actor. I'll tell you what I've done for her. One, I made her laugh; that was good for her. Two,

I made love to her; she liked that. Three, I made her pregnant; she didn't resent that as much as you seem to. Four, I tried to find her.'

'How did you try to find her?'

'I didn't report her to the cops. I don't report things to the cops.' He made his cop gesture with the finger a policemen broke when Roger was a good communist of seventeen. 'I looked for her all over town, wired her friends, so get your evidence right before you hang me.' Roger wasn't amusing himself. His eyes had widened, his voice was held most fiercely in control.

'You think I should have found her and married her? Crane, I've taught you nothing at all. You can really picture the roses banging against the cottage wall, the door painted green as a bean. And Roger Blester, his son on his lap, telling stories in which the giant always wins in the first round and honest Jack ends hanging like a dead pod from the beanstalk. And Beauty kisses the Beast and turns into a beast herself.'

'What about Elspeth?'

'She's dead.'

'Go to hell.'

He laughed—a rare, ugly sound.

'Johnny. You can't love if you can't hate—'

'Just what do you love, then?'

'Honesty,' he shouted, then turned it quickly into a gag. 'It's a very pretty little flower is Honesty.'

'Elspeth.'

Again he shut his eyes. Then he stuck out his right arm, the hand at the end of it bent back. It looked like a friendship gesture he had rehearsed for special occasions, like capture by the Japs.

'I'll buy you a drink, Johnny.'

'Go and eat Cheese Fancies.'

'I'll buy you two drinks, come on. Come and talk to me. Drink is the experience which erases all others. It makes the world go round and round.'

'I drank enough tonight.'

'Last chance, last chance of a drink with Bishop Blester?'
I thought of dull Elspeth, said 'Go to hell,' and left him
on his turret. But laughter always catches up with me.
Half way down the fire escape I caught myself laughing
again; careful analysis revealed the joke. My dinner-jacket
belonged to the theatre, now I was using it for a rooftop
scramble. That's what happens. I try to be fastidious and
then I get tight to the point where nonchalance becomes
impossible to maintain or even pronounce. Always in the
wrong clothes. If I played Henry VII at Stratford you'd
find me in the Avon, paddling in my Coronation robes.
My laughter slowed down. There were heavy-footed
dancers in my head. The window I found was not the
Mayor's window, but I liked the thought that one should
never retrace one's own steps. Then it became disturbing
to think of myself as 'one'. I could see a fantastic arrangement of stars, the tune of a band tapping at my ears,
transparent clouds walking across the sky. Does a condemned man watch the sky? Who else would bother? If
that sky could have rained it would have rained mercy.

Indoors again, I shook my head violently and it stayed
on. I washed away the blood in a basin, I combed my
hair, the comb soothed my scalp. But as I grew cleaner
and more respectable, my thoughts were jumping back to
the jungle. People who talk about suicide never do it,
they say, until the inquest. I never talk about it for it is
too important to me, a right, a secret fire exit which is
aways comfortingly available. I argued it out. Would a
propaganda note to say I did it because of the hanging
have any effect? They, especially Devon who could prove
it, would say I was unbalanced. I am unbalanced. I see
too much. It's an honest sort of madness. Suicide would
convert nobody. It was hard to see beyond the end of
McAllen, but there was Sheila, prepared to take on an
outrageous mad singer who took nothing seriously but his
own internal pictures of human suffering.

Plodding down the stairs to the plain of the public floor,
I had the sense to rest my stabbed hand in my pocket and

to leave the knife, intricately washed, in a lavatory cistern where it could rust. I was ordering at the bar when I heard a stockbroker voice behind me say:

'Dammit, the feller's got mud all down the back of his D.J. I say!'

'Get yourself stuffed,' I said, without turning round.

'I say—'

I turned and it was Ben. Without flickering, we continued the argument until people moved away. Then we launched into 'The Old Gags Are the Best Gags', a number rehearsed on many beer-breathed evenings. Some nice little girls in pink steered their gruff escorts round us as if we were a cabaret. We pounded into our farewell song:

> 'Cheerio, chaps, cheerio,
> We hope you all enjoyed our show,
> Find your toppers if you can,
> Don't forget to tip the cloakroom man.
> Cheerio, girls, cheerio,
> Terribly sorry that you have to go.
> With your escort shelter 'neath his great big brolly,
> And if he steals a little kiss it's jolly, jolly, jolly,
> Ta-ta, bye-bye and toodle-oo-doo,
> Good night, good luck, and right up you.'

There was some confusion as we finished, and a rugby forward capable of knocking our two heads together with one hand bought us drinks. It was time for Ben's trio again, I joined them on the stand. Ben was ready to drop his head on the keys in a solid 10,400-bar faint, but it was his hands which dropped, and sprung out of a long chord into a rhythm which bit across the ballroom. He nodded at me four times quickly, so I took the mike, holding it at a safe distance while I roared the blues:

> 'I was born in an ashcan, raised in a saloon,
> Yes, I was born in an ashcan, raised in a lousy saloon,
> Only thing I learnt was to yell the blues in tune.

'I was late being born, 'bout ten years overdue,
Well, the doctor said I was ten years overdue,
I'll be late for my death, but I'll never be late for you.

'So come early, baby, when you're through with your
     working day,
Come early, honey, when you get through that long, long
     day,
If you come late, God knows I may be taken away.

'Come early, come early, run to my crazy bed,
Won't you please come early, come to my crazy bed,
Make the terrible blues stop walkin' round my head.

'Come early, come early, come early, won't you hurry on,
Come early—hurry on,
Or you'll walk up the stairs and find your rider has gone.

'Now if anyone asks you, who sung this crazy song,
Anyone says: "Who sung that lousy song?"
Tell 'em Johnny Crane came early, but now that poor
     boy's gone.'

That poor boy's gone. That poor boy's gone. Elspeth,
unreported Elspeth, lost and gone. Four yards away stood
the Chief Constable. He had not been moving many
muscles since the photograph. When he recognized me he
said:

'Balmy evening, isn't it?'

I have a punch line for every cop remark, but I was
concerned with Elspeth.

'How do I report a missing person?'

He put his head on one side. It did not suit him. Even
when he held it upright his head did not suit him.

'You can tell me about it here.'

'It's a girl called Elspeth Gary. She was working at the
Acorn—'

'There's no harm in my telling you,' he said. 'Were you a

close friend of hers? It'll be in the papers tomorrow, of course. The morning papers.'

'Yes, a friend, just a friend,' I said vaguely. I remembered his lines from a sub-Christie play and I wanted the cutain to drop.

'She was found strangled in a ditch near Aberdeen. She must have been murdered on Sunday or Monday.'

He told me just like that. The room got hot. I looked down, so my calculations would be obscured. Roger had been at the Unicorn Sunday night and Tuesday morning. Roger didn't do it.

'What was she doing in Aberdeen, for heaven's sake?'

'Her mother was taken to hospital there. Her father phoned her, asked her to come straight away. That was last week.'

'Someone ought to tell Roger Blester.'

'Her fiance? The barman. Yes, we told him this afternoon.'

The mass of dancers danced against me like a current, holding me away from the stairs. Three men not in evening dress pushed through from the street door to the Chief Constable. They told him how they found Roger on the pavement. A panting man in a broad hat had seen him standing on the turret. He had dived with his feet together, head back and arms outstretched, graceful for the fall, then jarred into an asymmetrical shape on the pavement. A policeman ran down the stairs. Roger's bar-jacket and shoes had been left on the roof. He left them like a cautious swimmer diving in to rescue someone. For one bloody night I stop caring about someone, refuse help, and over he goes.

The street was set on a slant, sometimes I could see it sharply in focus, walls of stone and stone under my feet. Each lamp shone at the centre of a circle of radiating yellow lines, as thin as a thousand golden wires. My legs stopped. I had forgotten to send the rhythmic signals down to keep them moving one after the other. I stood rubbing my face. To think, I had to talk aloud:

'Bleeding stopped, that bleeding stopped. It bleeding stopped. Bit drunk. I better go and help Roger. Velma.

140

No. No. That in a ditch, what's that thing in a ditch? Elspeth. I need help, thou needest help, he needs help, she needs help, we need help, you need help, they need help.'

Devon's flat: the key was in the door, so I used it and went in. I could apologize to him, it would cost me something, but I had to pay. He was probably relaxing on his broad couch, getting up the strength to go to bed. As Devon let fly a long scream, I turned and ran for the street, down an alley, into another street. I had seen him relaxing on that broad couch. With him was Elsa. Devon was laying on his back, wearing only a purple-striped pyjama top. Elsa, dressed as a nannie, was putting a nappy on him. I had only come to explain, maybe to help, as everybody seemed to need help. But Devon could afford to buy the only help he needed. I nearly returned to tell him that I would keep my mouth shut.

The dawn in the sky was whitening and its coldness was exhilarating and clean. For an instant I felt so clean that I was transparent, my guts as white as that white light in the violet-edged sky. The street was like a great funnel pointing towards the sky, a megaphone for my good voice. I shouted 'I don't care.' The sound was pretty. I swung my arm so the injured hand might enjoy the air. At first it worked, then it failed, then I forgot my hand again. I was going slowly, tiring, as the light hardened round me. I heard myself say to the dust on my shoes 'I don't care,' and my eyes were so sore that they watered. There in front of me was a horse trough donated by a man who lived a long time ago. I sat on his memorial and cried for a bit, but it was controlled weeping. About fifty yards from Sheila's flat, if I touched the point of each railing spear with my hand it would be lucky. Then, without warning, the black rain in my head came down. I shook where I stood. I tensed, pulled myself forward by a railing, and ran to Sheila's. It would be the first time she had seen me chained down by madness. Like a TV set showing torture films to children in a nursery. I get messages from dead people. I get visions. I get more than my

141

share. I met a man who was unemployed and he wanted to be killed. They would have obliged him if there had been a war. But no one would kill him outright. I didn't kill him. They left him alone, we left him alone. Like Roger.

My feet had only one more thing to do. They took me to Sheila. She was sitting up for me, the scotch I did not want already poured for me. She looked after my hand. She said:

'How was it, love?'

'I don't know how it was, yes I do. It started well, it was golden. Then things happened, everything happened. Bad things. I don't know how it was, but now it's very bad.'

'What happened?'

'I can't talk about it. Stay here.'

'I'm not going. Do I make it any better?'

I began to laugh and discovered that I couldn't stop. She held me hard and helped me to stop.

'You'll see a doctor?'

'For my hand?'

'Not for your hand.'

'For my head? I don't want to. They make you talk about everything you don't want to talk about. I don't want to talk.'

'Johnny, listen to me. I'm not a nurse.'

'You don't want to live your life with a sick man.'

'Of course not. Have a little courage. Go and see a doctor tomorrow.'

'I could do that. But I'm not going in one of those places.'

'Don't be absurd, Johnny.'

'It's not absurd, you know I'm not being absurd. They put you in, and all the time you're looking at other mad people, and all the time they're looking at you. They have big eyes that look at you, mad people. You get madder in those places. And warders; they don't have real nurses, they have bloody warders.'

'What do you know about it?'

'I have dreams, you see.'

142

'And I've got friends who've been in mental hospitals and they're not like that. They got on all right.'

'They got out?'

'That's right. And it's not like that at all.'

'But I'm not going in.'

'Of course you're not. You're not mad. A bit sick.'

'A bit sick. I'll see a doctor. If you'll stay with me.'

'Don't make conditions. I'm not making any. I'll stay with you anyway.'

'I'll see a doctor. Yes. And I'll give Ford singing lessons.'

'Who's Ford?

'I never told you. Ford's my brother. You must meet him.'

There was a very long pause. First I looked at her and she didn't look at me. Then she looked at me and I didn't look at her.

'How is it, Johnny? How's your head?'

'It's beginning. I don't know. Are you ready? I don't know what's going to happen this time.'

'All right, Johnny, all right.'

She soothed me, cooled me, brought me pills. It only lasted an hour. I was asleep when we hung McAllen.

THE END